SMITHSONIAN INSTITUTION

UNITED STATES NATIONAL MUSEUM

BULLETIN 222

WASHINGTON, D.C.
1962

UNITED STATES GOVERNMENT PRINTING OFFICE, WASHINGTON, 1962

For sale by the Superintendent of Documents, U.S. Government Printing Office
Washington 25, D.C.

John Baptist Jackson:

18th-Century Master
of the Color Woodcut

Jacob Kainen

CURATOR OF GRAPHIC ARTS

MUSEUM OF HISTORY AND TECHNOLOGY

Publications of the United States National Museum

The scholarly publications of the United States National Museum include two series, *Proceedings of the United States National Museum* and *United States National Museum Bulletin.*

In these series are published original articles and monographs dealing with the collections and work of the Museum and setting forth newly acquired facts in the fields of Anthropology, Biology, History, Geology, and Technology. Copies of each publication are distributed to libraries and scientific organizations and to specialists and others interested in the different subjects.

The *Proceedings,* begun in 1878, are intended for the publication in separate form, of shorter papers. These are gathered in volumes, octavo in size, with the publication date of each paper recorded in the table of contents of the volume.

In the *Bulletin* series, the first of which was issued in 1875, appear longer, separate publications consisting of monographs (occasionally in several parts) and volumes in which are collected works on related subjects. *Bulletins* are either octavo or quarto in size, depending on the needs of the presentation. Since 1902 papers relating to the botanical collections of the Museum have been published in the *Bulletin* series under the heading *Contributions from the United States National Herbarium.*

This work forms number 222 of the *Bulletin* series.

REMINGTON KELLOGG
Director, United States National Museum

CONTENTS

	Page
Preface	IX
Jackson and his Tradition	3
The Woodcut Tradition	4
Status of the Woodcut	7
The Chiaroscuro Tradition	9
Jackson and his Work	13
England: Obscure Beginnings	14
Paris: Perfection of a Craft	17
Venice: The Heroic Effort	25
England Again: The Wallpaper Venture	40
Critical Opinion	51
Postscript	54
Catalog	69
Prints by Jackson	71
Jackson's Workshop	90
Unverified Subjects	95
The Chiaroscuros and Color Woodcuts	97
Bibliography	171
Index to Plates	177
Index	181

PREFACE

JOHN BAPTIST JACKSON has received little recognition as an artist. This is not surprising if we remember that originality in a woodcutter was not considered a virtue until quite recently. We can now see that he was more important than earlier critics had realized. He was the most adventurous and ambitious of earlier woodcutters and a trailblazer in turning his art resolutely in the direction of polychrome.

To 19th century writers on art, from whom we have inherited the bulk of standard catalogs, lexicons, and histories—along with their judgments—Jackson's work seemed less a break with tradition than a corruption of it. His chiaroscuro woodcuts (prints from a succession of woodblocks composing a single subject in monochrome light and shade) were invariably compared with those of the 16th century Italians and were usually found wanting. The exasperated tone of many critics may have been the result of an uneasy feeling that he was being judged by the wrong standards. The purpose of this monograph, aside from providing the first full-length study of Jackson and his prints, is to examine these standards. The traditions of the woodcut and the color print will therefore receive more attention than might be expected, but I feel that such treatment is essential if we are to appreciate Jackson's contribution, in which technical innovation is a major element.

Short accounts of Jackson have appeared in almost all standard dictionaries of painters and engravers and in numerous historical surveys, but these have been based upon meager evidence. A fraction of his work was usually known and details of his life were, and still are, sparse. Later writers interpreting the comments of their predecessors have repeated as fact much that was conjecture. The picture of Jackson that has come down to us, therefore, is unclear and fragmentary.

If he does not emerge from this study completely accounted for from birth to death, it has not been because of lack of effort. Biographical data for his early and late life—about fifty years in all—are almost entirely missing despite years of diligent search. As a man he remains a shadowy figure. I have traced Jackson's life as far as the available evidence will permit, quoting from the writings of the artist and his contemporaries at some length to convey an essential flavor, but I have refrained from filling in gaps by straining at conjecture.

While details of his life are vague, sufficient information is at hand to reconstruct his personality clearly enough. After all, Jackson wrote a book and was quoted at length in another. A contemporary fellow-practitioner wrote about him with considerable feeling. These and other sources give a good indication of the artist's character.

The man we have to deal with had something excessive about him; he was headstrong, tactless, impractical, enormously energetic, a prodigious worker, a conceiver of grandiose projects, and a relentless hunter of patrons. He was at home with his social superiors and had some pretentions to literary culture, he had a coarse gift for the vivid phrase in writing, and his tastes in art ran to the classic and heroic.

This study includes an illustrated catalog of Jackson's chiaroscuros and color prints. Previous catalogs, notably those of Nagler, Le Blanc, and Heller, have listed no more than twenty-five works. The present catalog more than triples this number.

To acknowledge fully the assistance given by museum curators, librarians, archivists, and scholars on both sides of the Atlantic would necessitate a very long list of names. However, I wish especially to thank Mr. Peter A. Wick of the Museum of Fine Arts, Boston, who has been generous enough to allow me to read his well-documented paper on Jackson's Ricci prints; Mr. A. Hyatt Mayor of the Metropolitan Museum of Art; Mr. Carl Zigrosser of the Philadelphia Museum of Art; Miss Anna C. Hoyt and Mrs. Anne B. Freedberg of the Museum of Fine Arts, Boston; Dr. Jakob Rosenberg and Miss Ruth S. Magurn of the Fogg Art Museum; Mr. Karl Kup of the New York Public Library; Miss Elizabeth Mongan of the Rosenwald Collection, National Gallery of Art; Miss Una E. Johnson of the Brooklyn Museum; Mr. Gustave von Groschwitz of the Cincinnati Art Museum; and Dr. Philip W. Bishop of the U.S. National Museum, Smithsonian Institution.

I am particularly grateful to curators of European collections, who have been uniformly generous in their assistance. Special thanks are due Mr. J. A. Gere of the British Museum and Mr. James Laver of the Victoria and Albert Museum, who have gone to considerable trouble to acquaint me with their great collections. Others whose help must be particularly noted are Mr. Peter Murray, Courtauld Institute of Art, University of London; Mme. R. Maquoy-Hendrickx of the Bibliothèque Royale de Belgique, Brussels; Dr. Vladimír Novotný of the Národní Galerie, Prague; Dr. Wegner of the Graphische Sammlung, Munich; Dr. Wolf Stubbe of the Kunsthalle, Hamburg; Dr. G. Busch of the Kunsthalle, Bremen; Dr. Hans Möhle of the Staatliche Museen, Berlin; Dr. Menz of the Staatliche Kunstsammlungen, Dresden; Miss B. L. D. Ihle of the Boymans Museum, Rotterdam; and M. Jean Adhémar of the Bibliothèque Nationale, Paris.

The excellent collections of chiaroscuro prints in the Museums of the Smithsonian Institution have formed a valuable basis for this monograph. These prints include the set of Jackson's Venetian chiaroscuros, originally owned by Jackson's patron, Joseph Smith, British Consul in Venice, now in the Rosenwald Collection, National Gallery of Art, and the representative sampling of Jackson's work in the Division of Graphic Arts, U.S. National Museum.

I am indebted to the following museums which have kindly given permission to reproduce Jackson prints in their collections. These are listed by catalog number.

    Smithsonian Institution 16, 18, 19, 20, 21, 22 (also in color), 24, 25, 26, 27, 28, 29, 30, 39, 50, 51, 52, 53 (also in color), 54, 55, 56, 57, 58, 63

    Museum of Fine Arts, Boston (W. G. Russell Allen Estate) 1 (also in color), 11, 14, 23, 33, 34, 38, 40 (also in color)

    Fogg Art Museum 13 (also in color)

    Worcester Art Museum 32

    Metropolitan Museum of Art 5 (Rogers Fund) (also in color), 17, 31 (gift of Winslow Ames), 73 (Whittelsey Fund)

    Philadelphia Museum of Art (John Frederick Lewis Collection) 2, 60, 61, 62, 64, 65, 66, 67, 68, 74

    British Museum 2 (in color), 6, 7, 8, 9, 10, 12, 15, 37, 41, 42, 43 (also in color), 44, 45, 46, 47, 48, 49 (also in color), 59, 69, 70, 71, 72, 75, 76 (photographs by John R. Freeman & Co.)

Victoria and Albert Museum (Crown copyright) 3, 35, 36, 40

Finally, I want to thank the Editorial Office of the Smithsonian Institution for planning and designing this book; the Government Printing Office for their special care in its production; and Mr. Harold E. Hugo for his expert supervision of the color plates.

A grant from the American Philosophical Society (Johnson Fund), made it possible to conduct research on Jackson in Europe. Acknowledgment is herewith gratefully given.

JACOB KAINEN
Smithsonian Institution

September 1, 1961

John Baptist Jackson

18th-Century Master
of the Color Woodcut

Jackson and His Tradition

The Woodcut Tradition

ALTHOUGH the woodcut is the oldest traditional print medium it was the last to win respectability as an art form. It had to wait until the 1880's and 1890's, when Vallotton, Gauguin, Munch, and others made their first unheralded efforts, and when Japanese prints came into vogue, for the initial stirrings of a less biased attitude toward this medium, so long considered little more than a craft. With the woodcut almost beneath notice it is understandable that Jackson's work should have failed to impress art historians unduly until recent times. Although he bore the brunt as an isolated prophet and special pleader between 1725 and 1754, his significance began to be appreciated only after the turn of the 20th century, first perhaps by Martin Hardie in 1906, and next and more clearly by Pierre Gusman in 1916 and Max J. Friedländer in 1917, when modern artists were committing heresies, among them the elevation of the woodcut to prominence as a first-hand art form. In this iconoclastic atmosphere Jackson's almost forgotten chiaroscuros no longer appeared as failures of technique, for they had been so regarded by most earlier writers, but as deliberately novel efforts in an original style. The innovating character of his woodcuts in full color was also given respectful mention for the first time. But these were brief assessments in general surveys.

If the woodcut was cheaply held, it was at least acceptable for certain limited purposes. But printing pictures in color, in any medium, was considered a weakening of the fiber—an excursion into prettification or floridity. It was not esteemed in higher art circles, except for a short burst at the end of the 18th century in France and England. This was an important development, admittedly, and the prints were coveted until quite recently. They are still highly desirable. But while Bartolozzi stipple engravings or Janinet aquatints in color might have commanded higher prices than Callots or Goyas, or even than many Dürers and Rembrandts, no one was fooled. The extreme desirability of the color prints was mostly a matter of interior decoration: nothing could give a finer 18th century aura. It was not so much color printing that mattered; it was *late 18th century* color printing that was wanted, often by amateurs who collected nothing else.

Color prints before and after this period did not appeal to discriminating collectors except as rarities, as exotic offshoots. Even chiaroscuros, with their few sober tones, fell into this periphery. Jackson, as a result, was naturally excluded from the main field of attention.

The worship of black-and-white as the highest expression of the graphic arts [1] automatically placed printmakers in color in one of two categories: producers of abortive experiments, or purveyors of popular pictures to a frivolous or sentimental public. This estimate was unfortunately true enough in most cases, true enough at least to cause the practice to be regarded with suspicion. As an indication of how things have changed in recent years we can say that color is no longer the exception. It threatens, in fact, to become the rule, and black-and-white now fights a retreating battle. A comparison of any large exhibition today with one of even 20 years ago will make this plain.

At first glance Jackson seems to be simply a belated 18th-century worker in the chiaroscuro process. If to later generations his prints had a rather odd look, this was to be expected. Native qualities, even a certain crudeness, were expected from the English who lacked advantages of training and tradition. And Jackson was not only the first English artist who worked in woodcut chiaroscuro, he was virtually the first woodblock artist in England to rise beyond anonymity [2] (Elisha Kirkall, as we shall see, cannot positively be identified as a wood engraver) and he was the only one of note until Thomas Bewick arose to prominence about 1780. He was, then, England's first outstanding woodcutter. We will find other instances of his significance from the English standpoint, but his being English, of course, would have a small part in explaining the importance of his prints.

Jackson made, in fact, the biggest break in the traditions of the woodcut since the 16th century. He broadened the scope of the chiaroscuro print and launched

---

[1] The purist's attitude was pungently expressed by Whistler. Pennell records this remark: "Black ink on white paper was good enough for Rembrandt; it ought to be good enough for you." (Joseph Pennell, *The Graphic Arts,* Chicago, 1921, p. 178.)

[2] The only earlier name is that of George Edwards. Oxford University has most of the blocks for a decorated alphabet he engraved on end-grain wood for Dr. Fell in 1674. Further data on Edwards can be found in Harry Carter's *Wolvercote Mill,* Oxford, 1957, pp. 14, 15, 20, and in Moxon's *Mechanick Exercises, or the Doctrine of Handy Works Applied to the Art of Printing.* (Reprint of 1st ed., 1683, edited and annotated by Herbert Davis and Harry Carter, Oxford, 1958, p. 26n.)

the color woodcut as a distinct art form that rivaled the polychrome effects of painting while retaining a character of its own. These were not modest little pieces of purely technical interest. The set of 24 sheets reproducing 17 paintings by Venetian masters made up the most heroic single project in chiaroscuro, and the 6 large landscapes, completed in 1744, after gouache paintings by Marco Ricci, were the most impressive color woodcuts in the Western world between the 16th century and the last decade of the 19th.

But Jackson's grand ambition to advance the woodcut beyond all other graphic media had little public or private support and finally led him to ruin. His efforts were made with insufficient means and with few patrons. As a consequence, he rarely printed editions after the blocks were cut and proofed. The Venetian set is well known because it was printed in a substantial edition. A few additional subjects were also sponsored by patrons, but most of Jackson's other chiaroscuros were never published—they were limited to a few proofs. Editions were postponed, no doubt, in the hope that a patron would come along to pay expenses in return for a formal dedication in Latin, but this did not often happen. Most subjects exist in a few copies only; of some, single impressions alone remain. Others have entirely disappeared.

With a large part of Jackson's work unknown, his reputation settled into an uneasy obscurity which, it must be granted, has not prevented his work from being collected. The chiaroscuros, especially the Venetian prints, can be found in many leading collections in Europe and the United States, but the full-color sheets after Ricci are excessively rare, particularly in complete sets.

Jackson has long been considered an interesting figure. His *Essay on the Invention of Engraving and Printing in Chiaro Oscuro . . .*,[3] with its bold claims to innovation and merit, his adventurous career as an English woodcutter in Europe, his adaptation of the color woodcut to wallpaper printing and his pioneering efforts in this field, and Papillon's immoderate attack on him in the important *Traité historique et pratique de la gravure en bois*[4] will be discussed later. For the moment we can say that the *Essay* was the first book by an Englishman with

---

[3] Jackson, London, 1754. Hereafter cited as *Essay*. Other references bearing directly on Jackson will receive only partial citation in the text. They are given in full in the bibliography, page 171.

[4] Papillon, Paris, 1766. Hereafter cited as the *Traité*.

color plates since the *Book of St. Albans* of 1486, with its heraldic shields in three or four colors, and the first book with block-print plates in naturalistic colors.[5]

Although critics have been interested in Jackson as an historical figure, they have been uncertain about the merit of his work. Opinions vary surprisingly. Most judgments were based on the Venetian chiaroscuros and depended upon the quality of impressions, many of which are poor. Criticisms when they have been adverse have been surprisingly harsh. It is unusual, to say the least, for writers to take time explaining how bad an artist is. To do this implies, in any case, that he warrants serious attention; space in histories is not usually wasted on nonentities. We can see now that Jackson was misunderstood because the uses of the woodcut were rigidly circumscribed by tradition.

Status of the Woodcut

AFTER the 15th century the woodcut lost its primitive power and became a self-effacing medium for creating facsimile impressions of drawings and for illustrating and decorating books, periodicals, and cheap popular broadsides. At its lowest ebb, in the late 17th century, and in the 18th, it was used to make patterns for workers in embroidery and needlework and to supply outlines for wallpaper designs to be filled in later by "paper-stainers."

The prime deficiency of the woodcut as an art form lay in the division of labor which the process permitted. Draughtsmen usually drew on the blocks; the main function of the cutter was to follow the lines precisely and carefully. Small room existed for individual style or original interpretation; there was little in the technique to distinguish one cutter from another. In spite of these limitations,

---

[5] Occasional book illustrations in two or three colors, confined chiefly to initial letters and ornamental borders, appeared as early as the 15th century. Ratdolt in 1485 printed astronomical diagrams in red, orange, and black, and used similar colors in a Crucifixion in the *Passau missal* of 1494. The *Liber selectarum cantionum* of Senfel, 1520, however, has a frontispiece printed in a broad range of colors from more than four woodblocks. The design is attributed to Hans Weiditz.

gifted cutters could rise beyond the dead level of ordinary practice. As fine draughtsmen with a feeling for their materials they did not trace with the knife, they drew and carved with it. Their feeling for line and shape was sensitive, crisp, and supple. But although they created the masterpieces of the medium they suffered from the traditional contempt for their craft. Creative ability in a woodcutter was rarely recognized, and the art fell into gradual decline. By the time the 18th century opened it had been almost entirely abandoned as a means of creating and interpreting works of art, and had been relegated to a minor place among the print processes.

The attitude of the print connoisseur was clearly stated as early as 1762 by Horace Walpole:[6]

> I have said, and for two reasons, shall say little of wooden cuts; that art never was executed in any perfection in England: engraving on metal was a final improvement of the art, and supplied the defects of cuttings in wood. The ancient wooden cuts were certainly carried to a great heighth, but that was the merit of the masters, not of the method.

William Gilpin in 1768 went even further. Describing the various contemporary print processes he omitted the woodcut entirely as not worthy of consideration. He acknowledged that "wooden cuts" were once executed by early artists but made no additional reference to the medium.[7]

As late as 1844 Maberly[8] cautioned print amateurs to steer clear of block prints:

> Prints, from wooden blocks, are much less esteemed, or, at least, are, generally speaking, of greatly less cost than engravings on copper; and there are connoisseurs who may, perhaps, consider them as rather derogatory to a fine collection.

Specialized histories of wood engraving, written mainly by 19th-century practitioners and bibliophiles, have tended to emphasize literal rendition rather than artistic vision. The writers favored wood engraving executed with the burin on the end grain of hard dense wood, such as box or maple, because it could produce

---

[6] Walpole, 1765 (1st ed. 1762), p. 3.
[7] William Gilpin, *An Essay on Prints,* London, 1781 (1st ed. 1768), p. 47. "There are three kinds of prints, engravings, etchings, and mezzotintos."
[8] Maberly, 1844, p. 130.

finer details than the old woodcut, which made use of knife and horizontally grained wood. They judged by narrow craft standards concerned with exact imitation of surface textures. Linton, for example, is almost contemptuous in his references to the chiaroscuro woodcut:[9]

> ... The poorest workman may suffice for an excellent chiaroscuro. I do not depreciate the artistic value as chiaroscuros of the various prints here noted nor underestimate the difficulty of production; but my business has been solely with the not difficult knifecutting and graver cutting of the same.

The Chiaroscuro Tradition

THE CHIAROSCURO woodcut was originally designed to serve a special purpose, to reproduce drawings of the Renaissance period. These were often made with pen and ink on paper prepared with a tint or with brush and wash tones on white or tinted paper. Highlights were made and modeled with brush and white pigment; the result had something of a bas-relief character. Neither line engraving nor etching was suited to reproducing these spirited drawings, but the chiaroscuro woodcut could render their effects admirably. Its nature, therefore, was conceived as fresh and spontaneous, as printed drawing, in fact.

Chiaroscuros were usually of two types, the German and the Italian. The Germans specialized in reproducing line drawings made on toned paper with white highlights. The woodcuts, however, could stand by themselves as black-and-white prints; the tones required separate printing. The typical German chiaroscuro was therefore from two blocks. The earliest dated print in this style is Lucas Cranach's *Venus,* with "1506" appearing on the black block. But the brown tint

---

[9] Linton, 1889, p. 215. A woodcut in the German manner was far more difficult to manage than Linton imagined. Bewick tried to imitate the cross-hatched lines of a Dürer woodcut without success. He finally concluded (1925, pp. 205–207) that the old woodcutters had used two blocks, each with lines going in opposing directions, and had printed one over the other!

might have been added a few years later. Jost de Negker, working after drawings by Hans Burgkmair, cut blocks which are dated, on the black block at least, as early as 1508, and work by Hans Baldung and Hans Wechtlin appeared shortly after.

The Italian style originated with Ugo da Carpi, who in 1516 petitioned the Senate in Venice to grant him exclusive rights to the chiaroscuro process, which he claimed to have invented. For many years, until Bartsch adduced proof in favor of the Germans, da Carpi was conceded to be the founder of this process. His first work dates from 1518 but obviously he produced prints earlier—how much earlier is uncertain. Working mainly after the loose, fresh wash drawings of Raphael and Parmigianino he developed a method of reducing their tonal constituents to two or three simple areas plus a partial outline, each of which was cut on a separate block. The blocks were then inked with transparent tones and printed one over the other to achieve gradations. White highlights were imitated, as in the German manner, by cutting out lines on a tone block to let the white paper assert itself. The result was a broadly treated facsimile of the original drawing. Some liberties were occasionally taken in interpretation, and sometimes fanciful changes were made in color combinations.

This technique was followed in Italy during the remainder of the 1500's, the most prominent early workers being Antonio da Trento (Fantuzzi), Domenico Beccafumi, and Giuseppe Niccolò Vicentino. Late in the century Andrea Andreani acquired a large number of blocks by previous Italian chiaroscurists and reissued them, adding his own monogram. By multiplying these subjects he reduced their rarity and emphasized their distinct character, their difference from other types of prints. The Italian term "chiaroscuro," meaning light and dark, has persisted as a generic name for this class of work.

The Italian and German techniques were often pursued in variant styles. The Germans sometimes used three blocks, with outlines not only in black but in a tone and white as well. Burgkmair's *Death as a Strangler* (B. 40)[10] and Wechtlin's *Alcon Freeing his Son from the Serpent* (B. 9) are of this type.

The Italians, in turn, often used two blocks in the German fashion, reproducing a complete crosshatched pen drawing with one tint block. Even da Carpi used this procedure more than occasionally, as in *St. John Preaching in the Desert*

---

[10] Adam Bartsch, *Le Peintre graveur,* Vienna, 1803–1821.

after Raphael (B. XII), and in *The Harvest* after Giulio Romano (B. XII). Most other Italian chiaroscurists made frequent use of this method which had the virtue of simplicity. Outstanding exponents included Niccolò Boldrini, who worked chiefly after drawings by Titian, and in the early 17th century the brothers Bartolomeo and G. B. Coriolano. Andreani's prints were usually in a more independent style which employed a clear outline in gray or soft brown with three tints blocks. While technical procedures were identical in Italian and German chiaroscuros after pen drawings, the Italian work tended to be looser than the German, which was more careful and methodical.

The Italian style, then, strictly interpreted, was simply the da Carpi style. Less rigorously considered, it included the free Italian variants of the German process.

Hendrick Goltzius of Haarlem, whose first chiaroscuros date from 1588, combined both Italian and German influences with marvelously crisp drawing and cutting and sharper color combinations than were common. Paulus Moreelse, a Dutch artist in the first half of the 17th century, employed a dark block in clear outline but modeled his forms internally in the da Carpi manner. The technical procedure was therefore close to Andreani's.

A number of other well-known artists including Simon Vouet and Christoffel Jegher, and quite a few anonymous ones, also turned out occasional pieces in the first half of the 17th century, generally in the manner of da Carpi or Goltzius. Perhaps the most prolific was Ludolph Businck, who created prints in France especially after drawings by George Lallemand.

After this period little was done in the medium until 1721, when Count Antonio Maria Zanetti in Venice made his first chiaroscuro woodcut. He worked consistently for almost thirty years and sent proofs to his friends in Europe, mostly important connoisseurs, through whom the prints became widely known. For the most part they were in the da Carpi style, to which he added a light charm. Between 1722 and 1724 Elisha Kirkall in London published twelve chiaroscuros after Italian masters. The prints were done in a combination of media—etching and mezzotint with relief blocks in either wood or metal—and were outside the woodcut tradition, but they attracted attention to the old process. In about 1726 Nicolas and Vincent Le Sueur in Paris produced some chiaroscuros, and a year later Jackson made his first example. The Le Sueurs followed da Carpi's method while Jackson used a loosely drawn outline and three tint blocks in a slight variation of the Andreani style.

One characteristic was shared in common by all early chiaroscurists; their work always reproduced drawings, usually in exact size. Jackson added a new dimension to the medium in 1735 by beginning to work after oil paintings.[11] His attempt to convey their scale, solidity, and tonal range, while retaining the woodcut's breadth of execution, was perhaps carrying the chiaroscuro into complexities for which it was not suited. The method called for extraordinary talents in planning, drawing, cutting, and printing, and it resulted in impressions that could not escape a certain heaviness of effect when compared with traditional work. Jackson's prints in this style are both daring and original, but no later woodcutter had either the desire or the temerity to follow his example. The method remained a dead end in chiaroscuro.

---

[11] Andrea Andreani in 1599 published ten plates after cartoons of Mantegna's nine paintings, *The Triumph of Julius Caesar* (B. 11), printed from four blocks in variations of gray. But Mantegna's cartoons were basically drawings in monochrome, and Andreani's fine chiaroscuros did not differ appreciably from the usual examples.

TAILPIECE in *L'Histoire naturelle éclaircie dans une de ses parties principales, l'oryctologie*, by D. d'Argenville, De Bure, Paris, 1755. This is one of the cuts Jackson made between 1725–1730. Actual size.

Jackson and His Work

England: Obscure Beginnings

LITTLE is known of Jackson's early years. It is assumed that he was born in England about 1700, although many accounts, probably based upon Nagler, have him born in 1701. Papillon[12] conjectures that he studied painting and engraving on wood with "an English painter" named "Ekwits," but is not sure he remembers the name correctly. He believes this artist engraved most of the head pieces and ornaments in Mattaire's *Latin Classics,* published by J. and R. Tonson and J. Watts in London, 1713, and remarks on similarities with Jackson's style. Chatto[13] believes these cuts were executed by Elisha Kirkall, interpreting the initials *EK* appearing on one of the prints to refer to this engraver rather than to "Ekwits." He goes on to assume that Kirkall also engraved the blocks for Croxall's edition of *Aesop's Fables,* 1722, by the same publisher, and adds that Jackson was probably his apprentice and might have had some share in their execution. Most accounts of Jackson, taking Chatto's word, note him as a pupil of Kirkall.

Linton[14] believes that only Kirkall or Jackson could have made the cuts, "unless some *Sculptor ignotus* is to be credited with that most notable book of graverwork in relief preceding the work of Bewick."

But it is doubtful that Jackson was a pupil of Kirkall. For this assumption we have the evidence of a curious and important little book, *An Enquiry into the Origins of Printing in Europe,*[15] which because of a misleading title and an anonymous author has been overlooked as a reference source. It is a transcription of Jackson's manuscript journal and was prepared for publication to coincide with

---

[12] Papillon, 1766, vol. 1, p. 323. Most probably Papillon confused "Ekwits" with Elisha Kirkall.

[13] Chatto and Jackson, 1861 (1st ed. 1839), p. 448.

[14] Linton, 1889, p. 130.

[15] London, 1752. Hereafter cited as the *Enquiry*. The first half deals with Jackson's opinions on the origins of printing from movable type and the progress of cutting on wood, the second half with Jackson's career and his venture into wallpaper manufacturing. The real content of the book was so little known that Bigmore and Wyman's comprehensive, annotated *Bibliography of Printing, London,* 1880-86, vol. 1, p. 201, described it as dealing with "certain improvements in printing-types made by Jackson, the typefounder."

the launching of the wallpaper venture. Kirkall is mentioned as follows (pp. 25–26):

> ... I shall give a brief account of the State of Cutting on Wood in England for the type Press before he [Jackson] went to France in 1725. In the beginning of this Century a remarkable Blow was given to all Cutters on Wood, by an invention of engraving on the same sort of Metal which types are cast with. The celebrated Mr. *Kirkhal,* an able Engraver on Copper, is said to be the first who performed a Relievo Work to answer the use of Cutting on Wood. This could be dispatched much sooner, and consequently answered the purpose of Book-sellers and Printers, who purchased these sort of Works at a much chaper [sic] Rate than could be expected from an Engraver on Wood ...

It does not seem reasonable that Jackson would learn the art of woodcutting from Kirkall and then refer to him as a famous engraver on copper and type metal. It is just as difficult to believe that Kirkall taught Jackson to work on metal, not wood.

The "EK" who engraved the blocks for Mattaire's *Latin Classics* might very well have been Kirkall, whose style also might have had something in common with Jackson's early work. But this would not necessarily indicate a definite influence. English pictorial relief prints for book illustration in the first decades of the 18th century had one characteristic in common; they were almost all done with the engraver's burin on type metal or end-grain boxwood. They therefore showed elements of a "white-line" style as opposed to the black-line or knife-cut method commonly used in other countries. While it is likely that Jackson was an exception to the general rule in England (we have his word for it in the *Enquiry,* as we shall see), he was also deeply influenced by the prevailing English style of burin work on wood or type metal. If Papillon saw a similarity between Jackson's cuts and those in the *Latin Classics,* it might have been because he was unfamiliar with other examples of English work and did not recognize a national style.

The initials "J. B. I." appear on a small cut in the 1717 edition of Dryden's plays, also published by Tonson. If this is an early piece by Jackson it would indicate that he might have been born earlier than 1701, although it is conceivable that he could have made it when he was sixteen.

This is the extent of the evidence, or rather lack of evidence, of Jackson's early years in England. Nothing is certain except that woodblock work was at a particularly low ebb. Standards in typography and printing were rude (Caslon was just beginning his career), far inferior to those on the Continent. Cuts were used rather sparingly by printers, and almost always for initial letters (these included little pictures), for tailpieces, and for decorative borders. As a measure of economy the same cut was often repeated throughout a book. Also, initial letters were sometimes contrived to permit the type for different capitals to be inserted in the center area, so that in some instances no more than two cuts were needed to begin alternate chapters in a volume. Rarely were woodblocks employed to illustrate the text. Pictures were almost always supplied by the copper-plate engraver, even when the prints were small and surrounded with typographical matter. This was an expensive and troublesome procedure, but it was the only one possible where an able group of cutters or engravers on wood did not exist and where printers found it difficult to achieve good impressions on the uneven laid paper of the time.

The main employment for knife cutters on wood was in making the popular prints, or illustrated broadsides, which had been sold in city and village throughout the country since the early 1600's. Plank and knife could be used for these prints because of the generally large size of the pictures and the lack of sophistication of the audience. They are described by Bewick from his memories as a boy in the 1760's:[16]

> I cannot, however, help lamenting that, in all the vicissitudes which the art of wood engraving has undergone, some species of it are lost and done away: I mean the large blocks with the prints from them, so common to be seen, when I was a boy, in every cottage and farm house throughout the country. These blocks, I suppose, from their size, must have been cut on the plank way on beech, or some other kind of close-grained wood; and from the immense number of impressions from them, so cheaply and extensively spread over the whole country, must have given employment to a great number of artists, in this inferior department of woodcutting . . . These prints, which were sold at a very low price, were commonly illustrative of some memorable exploits, or were, perhaps, the portraits of eminent men . . . Besides these, there were a great variety of other designs, often with songs added to them of a moral, a patriotic, or a rural tendency, which served to enliven

---

[16] Bewick, 1925 (1st ed. London, 1862), pp. 211–212.

the circle in which they were admired. To enumerate the great variety of these *pictures* would be a task.

Bewick adds that some of these popular woodcuts, although not the great majority, were very good. Since this was the main field for woodcutters, it is an interesting conjecture that Jackson might have been trained for this craft. As he matured, we can assume that he felt the urge to excel as a woodcutter and left the country to develop his potentialities.

It must be remembered that in painting and engraving England was far behind the continental countries, which could boast of centuries of celebrated masters. The medieval period persisted in England until the time of Henry VIII. Traditional religious subjects, so indispensable to European art, were thereafter generally proscribed. There was no fondness as yet for themes of classical mythology, and the new and developing national tradition in painting had to form itself on the only remaining field of pictorial expression, portraiture. Standards of style were set by foreign artists who were lured to England to record its prominent personages in a fitting manner. Beside such masters as Holbein, Zuccaro, Moro, Geeraerts, Van Dyck, Mytens, Lely, Kneller, Zoffany, and Van Loo, among others, native painters seemed crude and provincial. The list of foreign artists other than portraitists who visited England before 1750 for varying periods is also impressive.

If good native painters were rare in the first decades of the 18th century, good engravers or woodcutters were even rarer. Hogarth, whose earliest prints were produced in the 1720's, received his training from a silversmith.

Jackson's next move was toward the Continent.

Paris: Perfection of a Craft

JACKSON arrived in Paris in 1725, his age 24 if we accept 1701 as his birth date. Here flourished a brilliant community of artists, craftsmen, dealers, and connoisseurs; woodcutting, etching, and line engraving were highly developed and the printing offices made extensive use of woodcuts for decoration and illustration. The woodcut tradition mimicked line engraving and was confined chiefly to tiny blocks wrought with the utmost delicacy. The main influence came from the 17th century— in particular from the etchings and line engravings of Sébastien Le Clerc and from the etchings of Jacques Callot, whose simple system of swelling parallel lines, with occasional cross-hatchings, was adopted by both line engravers and woodcutters.

Le Clerc, whose style was influenced by Callot, had produced a vast number of illustrations involving subjects of almost every type; his designs, therefore, were ready-made for publishers who wanted good but low-priced illustrations. Woodcutters copied his engravings shamelessly, line for line. The overblown high Baroque style in ornament, swag, and cartouche was also drawn upon as a source for decorative cuts. In an attempt to imitate the full tonal scale of engraving, the woodcutters used heavier lines in the foreground to detach the main figures from the background, which was made up of more delicate lines. Background lines were often narrowed further by scraping down their edges, an operation that caused them to merge imperceptibly into the white paper. In this way, although the natural vigor of the woodcut suffered, an effect of space and distance was achieved. Because of the small scale this technique was difficult, especially when cross-hatching was added, and special knives as well as a phenomenal deftness were needed to work out these bits of jewelry on the plank grain of pear, cherry, box, and serviceberry wood.

Jackson's initial impression of the state of woodcutting in France is described in the *Enquiry* (p. 27):

> From this Account it is evident that there was little Encouragement to be hoped for in England to a Person whose Genius led him to prosecute his Studies in the ancient Manner; which obliged Mr. *Jackson* to go over to the Continent, and see what was used in the *Parisian* Printing-houses. At his arrival there he found the *French* Engravers on Wood working in the old Manner; no Metal Engravers, or any of the same Performance on the end of the Wood, was ever used or countenanced by the Printers or Booksellers in that City. He tells us that he thought himself a tolerable good Hand when he came to *Paris,* but far inferior to the Performances of Monsieurs *Vincent le Seur* and *Jean M. Pappillon . . .*

Jackson admits benefiting from the friendship and advice of these woodcutters, then goes on to describe their work with a ruthless frankness. Le Sueur, he says, was a brilliant copyist of the line engravings of Sébastien Le Clerc but, because he was a line-for-line copyist, lacked skill in drawing. Papillon's father, also a woodcutter who copied LeClerc, avoided cross-hatching, which Jackson considered an essential ingredient of the true style of black-and-white woodcutting; Papillon himself, while described as a draughtsman of the utmost accuracy, was criticized for making his work so minute that it was impossible to print clearly. Jackson says in the *Enquiry* (pp. 29–30):

> If his Father neglected Cross Hatching, the Son affected to outstrip the *le Seurs* in this difficult Performance, and even the ancient *Venetians,* believing to have fixed a *Non plus ultra* in our Times to any future Attempts with Engraving on Wood.
> ... I saw the Almanack [17] in a horrid Condition before I left *Paris,* the Signs of the Zodiack wore like a Blotch, notwithstanding the utmost Care and Diligence the Printer used to take up very little Ink to keep them clean. I have chosen to make mention of these two *Frenchmen* as the only Persons in my time keeping up to the Stile of the ancient Engraving on Wood; and as they favoured me with their Friendship and Advice during my abode in *Paris,* I thought in Justice to their good Nature it was proper to give some Account of their Merit!

Acknowledgment of friendship and merit in this vein, while entirely true (Papillon was minute to the point of exhibitionism, and his cuts were often not adapted to clear printing), demonstrates the lack of tact that made powerful enemies for Jackson wherever he traveled. Papillon no doubt read the *Enquiry,* in which he was discussed at length, and the well-known *Essay,* with its aggressive tone and irresponsible claims. When Papillon's *Traité* came out in 1766 he took the opportunity to put the English artist in his place. Certainly his account was colored by Jackson's writings; there is no other explanation for this display of personal bitterness in a work published 36 years after the Englishman left Paris (pp. 327–328):

> J. Jackson, an Englishman who lived in Paris for a few years, might have perfected himself in wood engraving, which he had learned, as I said previously on page 323, from an English painter, if he had been willing to follow my advice. As soon as he arrived in Paris he came to me asking for work; I gave him some things to execute for a few months in order to allow him to live, for which he repaid me with ingratitude by making a duplicate of a floral ornament of my design which he offered, before delivering the block to me, to the person for whom it was to be

---

[17] The *Petit almanach de Paris,* founded by J. M. Papillon in 1727 and illustrated with his woodcuts.

made. From the reproaches I received when the matter was discovered, I refused, naturally, to employ him further. Then he went the rounds of the printing houses in Paris, and was forced to offer his work ready-made and without order, almost for nothing, and many printers, profiting by his distress, supplied themselves amply with his cuts. He had acquired a certain insipid and limited taste, little above the mosaics on snuffboxes, similar to other mediocre engravers, with which he surcharged his works. His mosaics, however delicately engraved, are always lacking in effect, and show the engraver's patience and not his talent; for the remainder of the cut has only delicate lines without tints or gradations of light and shade, and lack the contrast necessary to make a striking effect. Engravings of this sort, however deficient in this regard, are admired by printers of vulgar taste who foolishly believe that they closely resemble copper plate engraving, and that they give better impressions than those of a picturesque type having a greater variety of tints.

Jackson, having been forced by poverty to leave Paris, where he could find nothing further to do, traveled in France; then, disgusted with his art, he followed a painter to Rome, after which he went to Venice, where, I am told, he married, and then returned to England, his native country.

Whether or not Jackson was unethical he was certainly an active competitor and many printers "supplied themselves amply with his cuts." He must have produced an enormous amount of work during his five years in Paris because John Smith, in his *Printers Grammar*,[18] says that Jackson's cuts were used so widely and for so many years in Paris that they replaced the fashion of using "flowers," or typographical ornaments, and that this style did not come into vogue again until the cuts were completely worn down through use.

This statement is not entirely true, but it is probable that Jackson's woodcuts, more broadly executed than the typical French products, outlasted all others of the 1725–30 period. They were consistently re-used, and appeared, as far as they can be traced, well into the 1780's.[19]

Elsewhere in the *Traité,* however, Papillon has a good word for Jackson's abilities:[20]

Jackson, of whom I have already spoken, also engraved in chiaroscuro; I have a little landscape by him which is very nicely done.

---

[18] Smith, 1755, p. 136.

[19] See cuts in *Dissertatiumeula quodlibetariis disputationibus* of C. L. Berthollet, Paris, 1780, and *Voyage littéraire de la Grèce,* of de Guys, 1783.

[20] P. 415. This may be the print formerly in Dresden but lost during the war.

It was inevitable that Papillon and Jackson should clash. The Frenchman's notion of woodcutting was influenced, as we have seen, by copper plate engraving; he wanted, by incredible minuteness of cutting, to achieve approximately the same results. This was in keeping with the delicate French *rocaille* tradition on which Papillon was nurtured; to him any other contemporary style of book decoration was evidence of bad taste. Jackson, on his part, felt that this approach violated the essentially broad, vigorous nature of the woodcut and, in addition, made excessive demands on the printer. Since this impoverished beginner, and an Englishman at that, refused to take his earnest advice or to fall into the prevailing style, Papillon

HEADPIECE by J. M. Papillon for his *Traité historique et pratique de la gravure en bois,* Paris, 1766, vol. 3. This is an example of Papillon's minute style, against which Jackson rebelled. Actual size.

was enraged. After all, Jackson was working as an employee. But Papillon was not entirely blind. In a number of places in the *Traité* he made reference to other woodcutters who were working in Jackson's style, and he recorded some of the works the Englishman illustrated during his five years in Paris.

Jackson's blossoming out as a maker of wallpaper after his return to England and his brash claims in this connection in the *Essay,* must also have irked Papillon, who knew the field as an expert; his father in 1688 had set up the first large printing house in France for wall hangings, and after his death in 1723 Papillon had inherited it. In 1740, he sold the business to the widow Langlois, but he had run the shop during Jackson's residence in Paris and his former employee no doubt had learned a great deal by observing its operation. Yet here more than twenty years later was the upstart Englishman again, venturing into wallpaper manufacturing with an air of moral superiority, attacking all other products as unworthy. Jackson's ridiculing of the Chinese style must have been particularly galling since

21

Papillon and his father had specialized in producing such papers. These were much better than comparable English work, but Jackson, confining himself to English products, had attacked the whole style without making distinctions.

According to the *Enquiry* (pages 32–55 of this book will be drawn upon for the ensuing details of Jackson's career), M. Annison, Director of the Imprimerie Royale, for whom Jackson produced many cuts, introduced him to Count de Caylus, collector, connoisseur, etcher, and the leading spirit in French engraving at the time. De Caylus had, in 1725, undertaken to direct the reproduction of drawings and paintings in the best French collections.[21] Pierre Crozat, the famous collector, sponsored the publication of this ambitious work.

The drawings were reproduced in chiaroscuro while the paintings were rendered in black-and-white by a corps of engravers. The chiaroscuros were made by combining an etched outline, usually by de Caylus or P. P. A. Robert, with superimposed tones, mainly in green or buff, from one or two woodblocks cut in most cases by Nicolas Le Sueur, or under his direction. This was not a new printing method. Hubert (not Hendrick) Goltzius had first employed it in a set of Roman emperors after antique medallions in 1557.[22] To reproduce drawings by Raphael, Parmigianino, and himself, Abraham Bloemart, as well as Frederick and Cornelius Bloemart in the early 1600's, had used this combination extensively, and as described earlier, p. 11, Kirkall had used it between 1722 and 1724.[23] The combination method produced rather feeble prints that lacked the vigor of straight woodblock chiaroscuro. The etched outline was thin and ineffective, and the tints were pallid so as not to overpower the drawing. Only Abraham Bloemart's prints in this style were convincing, although Kirkall's chiaroscuros, in their soft, overmodeled way, had individuality. But the *Cabinet Crozat* lacked distinction entirely. The chiaroscuros had a mechanical look, a fact not surprising when we remember that they were produced by a team of engravers—assembled, as it were,

---

[21] *Recueil d'estampes d'après les plus beaux tableaux et d'après les plus beaux dessins qui sont en France dans le cabinet du Roy, dans celui de M. le Duc d'Orléans et dans d'autres cabinets, divisé suivant les différentes écoles.* Paris, 1729–42, 2 vols., 182 plates. Often called the *Cabinet Crozat*, it was reprinted by Basan in 1763 with aquatint tones by François Charpentier replacing the woodblock tints.

[22] *Imperatorum imagines*, Antwerp, 1557. The woodblocks were cut by Josse Geitleugen.

[23] In the *Enquiry* (p. 31) Jackson asserts that Kirkall's tints were made from copper plates, not woodblocks.

from several hands working in different media. The best prints were a few chiaroscuros made entirely from woodblocks by Nicolas Le Sueur, although these were also rather tepid, no doubt to harmonize with the rest of the work.

Jackson tells us that he worked on some tint blocks, first from a drawing by Giulio Romano and later from a drawing by Raphael, *Christ Giving the Keys to St. Peter,* the original *modello* for one of the famous tapestry cartoons. Count de Caylus, he says, liked the work and wanted to employ him further on the project, but Crozat rejected him flatly. De Caylus, according to Jackson, was embarrassed and distressed and offered recompense for the lost time and labor, but Jackson, not to be outdone in generosity by a nobleman, refused, explaining that the honor of knowing the Count and receiving his approbation more than made up for his lost effort.

Vincent Le Sueur objected to the combination method and withdrew early from the project. Possibly Jackson, who also disliked this method and was not known for his discretion, was considered by Crozat to be a disruptive element. Possibly his style of cutting was not retiring enough for Crozat's tasteful French notion of chiaroscuro. This project, in any case, aroused the Englishman's interest in the process. *Christ Giving the Keys to St. Peter,* after Raphael, made about 1727, was probably Jackson's first chiaroscuro woodcut. No doubt he produced it on his own and offered it as a plate for the publication, perhaps at the time he was commissioned to cut the tint blocks to be used in combination with de Caylus' etching of this subject.

With both Papillon and the powerful Crozat against him, Jackson was finished in Paris. De Caylus urged him to go to Italy. Accordingly, in April 1730, he left Paris in the company of John Lewis, an English painter, and set out for Rome, where he expected to continue his studies in drawing and deepen his knowledge of art.

Jackson's style was still being formed during his Paris period. Confined for the most part to initial letters, headbands, and tailpieces, his work differed from contemporary French cuts only in its technical handling, which was firmer and broader. Little of a more creative nature came his way, and the Paris stay therefore served as a useful interim during which he became adept in his craft. The necessity for keeping himself alive by cutting on wood developed his powers of invention and his facility: he became a remarkably rapid and skillful cutter. Jackson gathered strength in Paris, but it was in Venice that he really came to maturity as an artist.

TAILPIECE in *Histoire générale de Languedoc*, by Claude Vic and J. J. Vaissete, Paris, 1730, vol. 1. Note the even tone and clean cutting compared with Papillon's light-and-dark contrasts and dainty cutting. Actual size.

Venice: The Heroic Effort

AFTER leaving Paris, Jackson and Lewis journeyed to Marseilles, where Jackson became seriously ill and remained for six months, while Lewis continued to Genoa. Regaining his health, Jackson went on to Genoa and then to Leghorn, Pisa, and Lucca, arriving in Florence in January 1731. There, during a stay of several months, he discussed with the Grand Duke of Tuscany a reprinting of Vasari's *Lives of the Painters*. Jackson was to make cuts for the headpieces, but the project was eventually dropped, and he continued to Bologna, where he remained a month chiefly in the company of the woodcutter G. M. Moretti, who showed him some original blocks cut by Ugo da Carpi for printing in chiaroscuro. He then proceeded to Venice, arriving "three Days before the Feast of the Ascension in 1731, and was highly surprized to find no one Engraver on Wood capable to do such poor Work, he has seen at Bolonia." Jackson was amply supplied with strong recommendations from Florence, and on showing his work to leading printers was urged to settle in Venice, where a fine woodcutter capable of both designing and executing cuts was urgently needed. Here he also met Count Antonio Maria Zanetti, who was well-known as a chiaroscuro woodcutter besides being a collector and patron of the arts. Their first meeting is described in the *Enquiry*:

> ... very soon after his [Jackson's] Arrival he had an Interview with Signior *Antonio Maria Zannetti;* from the Accounts he had heard from Mr. *Marriette* in *France* of this Man's Work in *Chiaro Oscuro,* he expected to see some wonderful Performance, but *Parturiunt montes nascetur ridiculus mus* is a most applicable Proverb on this Occasion. I who have perused this grand Raccolta of *Zannetti's,* must acknowledge that they are a trifling Performance, inferior to any Attempts of this Kind in our Times; and indeed it is no Wonder, when we come to know that this Man never used a Press, nor so much as a Hand Roll to print his Works with. Our Countryman says he had room to suspect he neither did cut or print these Works, which was confirmed by the poor Men who performed both. But such was the Vanity of this Author, that he told the Public in his Dedications that he was the Restorer of that lost Art, whereas he only drawed them on the Blocks,

which might have been done as well by those that cut and printed them. At this first Interview the low Cunning of this Man was discovered . . .[24]

Jackson undoubtedly disliked Zanetti's soft and delicate treatment, so characteristic of 18th-century work, and considered his interpretation of Parmigianino and Raphael little short of sacrilege. Since Jackson was incapable of hiding his feelings a quarrel became inevitable. The first rift came when Zanetti let Jackson have for a few weeks a drawing by Parmigianino, the *Venus and Cupid with a Bow*, to be executed in four blocks. The print was done "intirely in *Hugo's* [da Carpi's] manner, with this Difference, that no *Oscuro* block has a Contour to resemble the original Drawing it was done from, which is seldom seen in *Hugo's* works . . . ." Zanetti, surprised by the fine quality of the first proof, proposed to pass it off on Mariette in Paris as an original da Carpi print. He even stained it and cut holes in it to give the impression of aged worm-eaten paper. At the same time Jackson executed another chiaroscuro, also based on a Parmigianino drawing, the *Woman Standing Holding Jar on her Head*. Zanetti, says the *Enquiry*—

> . . . caressed the Author with the highest Expressions of Zeal for his Service, protesting he would communicate his Capacity to his Correspondents all over *Europe*, which would be the Means to advance his Fortune, especially amongst the *English* Quality and Gentry who travelled *Italy*. The intent of all those fine Promises was to get the two Sets of Blocks into his Hands, which he expected as a Present for the Use of the two original Drawings, from which these Prints were taken; but this not being complyed with, the *Restaurati* expressed a Resentment at this Refusal, and took all the Opportunities to distress the Undertakings of any Sort performed by Mr. *Jackson,* during fourteen Years Residence in *Venice*.

Zanetti was charged, in some obscure way, with obstructing Jackson's work in cutting 136 blocks for the *Istoria del Testamento Vecchio e Nuovo*, popularly known as the *Bibbia del Nicolosi*,[25] published by G. B. Albrizzi in 1737. We are informed that Filippo Farsetti, one of Jackson's patrons, paid him for the whole set of cuts after rebuking Zanetti for interference.

---

[24] Zanetti certainly cut many of his own blocks, as the prints with the signature "A. M. Zanetti, sculp." attest. But he also made use of craftsmen in the traditional fashion for other blocks and for the mechanical phase of printing.

[25] These cuts were also used for the *Biblia Sacra*, published by Hertz in Venice in 1740.

The Englishman evidently was kept well occupied with preparing cuts for printers, among them Baglioni and Pezzana. For the latter he made 24 woodcuts for a quarto edition of a *Biblia Sacra* and an unspecified number of ornaments for a folio edition. Jackson was given a free hand to conceive and carry out the cuts as he pleased.

While working on these prints he began—

> to consider on his favourite Work in *Chiaro Oscuro,* and by intervals examined what he had projected at *Paris*. He began first to make experiments with Tints, and having proved that Four Impressions could produce Ten positive Tints, besides *Tratti* and *Lights;* he resolved to try a large Piece from *Rubens's* Judgment of *Solomon,* with an intent to prove what could be done with the Efforts of a Type Press before he launched into greater Expences with another Machine.

He wanted this press in his home, where he could experiment as he pleased without tying up workmen or equipment in Pezzana's shop. It might have been professional delicacy that prompted him to ask Pezzana's permission to have a private press built, or it might have been a bid for patronage from the generous and influential printer. In any event, Pezzana responded by having his carpenters build and install the press at his own expense. To avoid official registrations or craft suspicions, he had it registered as his own. The trial proofs of *The Judgment of Solomon,* printed from four blocks, pleased Jackson in every regard except vigor of impression. Unfortunately no edition was published, despite the dedication to Filippo Farsetti.

Finished in 1735, this woodcut was probably the first to translate a painting in a full range of tones. From the purely technical standpoint it was an incredible achievement. Jackson created a vivid approximation of a large and complex painting and at the same time produced a vigorous woodcut. From four superimposed woodblocks, with almost no linework, he was able to capture the full-blooded forms of Rubens. By keeping his means simple Jackson asserted the importance of his cutting and printing, the expressiveness of his drawing, and the fluidity of his tones. Obviously such a procedure required major decisions as to what to omit and what to stress; in other words it required interpretive abilities of a high order.

Evidently Jackson believed that his new chiaroscuro method required heavier pressure than the platen press was capable of. (On the usual wooden screw press the size of the platen never exceeded 13 by 19 inches, because the impressions made with a larger platen would not have been strong enough; for prints larger than the platen, the bed was moved and the platen pulled down twice.) He had the press returned to Pezzana and set out to build a more suitable printing machine.

> He found there were other means to be employed beside a Type Press, and having examined the Theory of his Invention put it in Practice, by erecting a Rolling Press of another Construction than what is used for printing Copper Plates.

In Paris Jackson had suggested using a cylinder press for printing wood blocks. The gentlemen to whom the suggestion was made, Count de Caylus, Coypel, and Mariette, were sure that the enormous pressure would split the blocks. The Englishman, on the contrary, felt that the pressure, properly controlled by a chase, would hold the blocks together. Printing would be much more rapid and the exceptional vigor of the impression would suggest a hand drawing. The use of cylinder presses for chiaroscuro printing was already well known to experts. George Lallemand and Ludolph Businck, sometime between 1623 and 1640, had used not one but a series of six cylinders on three joined presses, with three printers simultaneously inking separate blocks with different tones. Impressions were then printed from each block in succession. Papillon[26] described this press, and also another with a special chase designed at an unspecified date by Nicolas Le Sueur. Jackson's prints show a much stronger impression than those of Businck or Le Sueur. No details of his press are known, although Thomas Bewick[27] reported that Jackson as an old man had shown him a drawing of its construction.

ILLUSTRATION in *Biblia Sacra* published by Hertz, Venice, 1740, vol. 1. Originally cut by Jackson for Albrizzi's *Istoria del Testamento Vecchio e Nuovo*, Venice, 1737. Actual size.

---

[26] Papillon, vol. 2, 1766, pp. 372–373.　　[27] Bewick, 1925, p. 213.

The cylinder press of Jackson's design was finished in 1735 and paid for by the income from prolonged sieges of work for printing offices. But the overwork and resulting exhaustion laid him low; a serious illness followed and for several months he was close to death. When he eventually regained his health he found that his cuts for Baglioni and Pezzana had been copied and mutilated by an engraver at Ancona. This pirate was encouraged by the head of a large printing establishment newly founded in Venice, who thereupon offered Jackson work at greatly reduced prices. He refused the offer. With hack woodcutters now stealing both his designs and his manner of cutting, and working at a far lower rate than he could afford, he found that the market for his higher priced work had almost entirely disappeared. He still received occasional commissions, among others the title page to a translation of Suetonius' *Lives of the Twelve Caesars,* printed by Piacentini in Venice in 1738. His splendid design, which shows considerable burin work, is at odds with the crudity of the remainder of the book. Inferior hands reproduced in woodcut outline Hubert Goltzius' medallion portraits of Roman emperors, originally executed in chiaroscuro (see p. 22). Stimulated, no doubt, by the combination of chiaroscuro and antiquity, Jackson produced a portrait of Julius Caesar in four tones of brown after Egidius Sadeler's engraving of a subsequently lost painting attributed to Titian. This was not the only time Jackson translated a line engraving and added chiaroscuro modeling of his own. He did not make line-for-line copies. Jackson was interested in broad effects even when leaning heavily on the delicate linear conventions of line engraving. The lines, therefore, are firm and

ILLUSTRATION for Albrizzi's *Istoria*, in which it was cut No. 136. From Hertz's *Biblia Sacra*, vol. 1. Actual size.

29

widely spaced, like photographically enlarged details of copper-plate work. Apparently Jackson felt that the addition of one or two tones from wood blocks would supply the intermediate tints and at the same time would prevent the line system from becoming obtrusive.

The decided influence of line engraving was probably the result of his association in 1731 with G. A. Faldoni in Venice. Influenced by Claude Mellan, this engraver made use of swelling parallel lines to create tonal gradations. Jackson had first become interested in this technical method through Ecman's woodcuts after Callot, and once Faldoni had strengthened the attraction he found kindred influences in the engravings of Villamena and Alberti, particularly the former, from whom he also acquired design ideas he later put to use in his wallpapers. Jackson's discovery that he could to some extent use copper-plate techniques was not a reversion to the style of the Parisian group of Le Clerc copyists. Jackson used the line system as a means for creating forms in conjunction with tones; the Parisian woodcutters used it to imitate the delicate quality of line engraving. He had a formal aesthetic end in view; their purpose was to render realistic details in a decorative framework.

With opportunities for book illustration gone, Jackson was in a difficult position. His novel chiaroscuro experiments had consumed valuable time and had lost him his standing as a steady worker for printers. Near destitution and scouting around for fresh applications of the woodcut, he decided to make prints for wallpaper on his new press. It was a logical step for Jackson, not only because he knew something of the process but also because he could make use of the chiaroscuro blocks already prepared. Late in 1737 or early in 1738 he had his first samples ready and sent them to Robert Dunbar in London, together with his conditions for carrying on the trade in Venice. Negotiations dragged, and Dunbar died before they could come to terms, but the idea of using his skill and his machine for turning out wallpaper continued to occupy his mind as a possibility. But, for the time, the undertaking had to be laid aside while Jackson looked for more immediate means of employment.

At this juncture Joseph Smith befriended him. A merchant of long standing in Venice, who became the British consul there in 1745, Smith was a bibliophile, gem collector, and connoisseur of the arts. In spite of Walpole's sneering reference to him as "the merchant of Venice," it must be said that he was expert in his fields of interest. He had excellent taste. His fine collection of books was purchased by George III in 1765, and the small Rembrandt *Descent from the Cross* once in his possession is now in the National Gallery in London.

From Smith's bronze statuette of Neptune, by Giovanni da Bologna, Jackson produced a chiaroscuro print in four blocks, in imitation, he asserted, of the prints of Andrea Andreani.[28] In suggesting the influence of this master, Jackson did not refer to his technique or style but to his subject: in 1584–1585 Andreani had produced a chiaroscuro series after other statues by Giovanni da Bologna (B. XII, VI, 1–4).

The next work in Smith's collection to be reproduced in chiaroscuro was Rembrandt's *Descent from the Cross*. Jackson was evidently well satisfied with the results, and with good reason. It is an extremely effective print, with pale yellow lights and transparent shadows. The drawing is remarkable in its feeling for the Rembrandtesque style. The sky and other parts show English white-line burin work of the type found in Mattaire's *Latin Classics* and Croxall's *Aesop's Fables*. The *Enquiry* says (p. 45):

> As this Painting was extremely favourable for this sort of Printing, he endeavoured to display all his Art in this Performance, and the Drawing of *Rembrandt's* Stile is intirely preserved in this Print; it is dedicated to Mr. *Smith,* who generously gave the Prints to all Gentlemen who came to *Venice* at that time in order to recommend the Talents of a Man whose Industry might please the curious, and at least be of some Use to procure him Encouragement to proceed in other Works of that Kind.

Encouragement soon came. Smith interested two of his friends, Charles Frederick and Smart Lethieullier, and the three proposed in 1739 the undertaking of a grand project in chiaroscuro, the reproduction of 17 huge paintings by Venetian masters. This was to be financed by subscription, says the *Enquiry* (p. 46):

---

[28] The *Neptune* was printed on a type press. One of the blocks split in printing and Jackson stated that thereafter he used the cylinder press exclusively.

the Proposals in *French,* and the Conditions expressed therein, were drawn up as they thought proper, without consulting the Difficulties that must attend an Enterprize that required some years to accomplish.

Their own subscriptions were no doubt generous but Jackson found that his total income from this form of financing, together with possible future sales, would hardly cover his expenses. Other hazards made his situation even worse. War broke out in Europe before he was halfway through, and many English gentlemen, his potential subscribers, left the country. This exodus meant financial disaster, but Jackson kept at his task. He should, he said, have gone to England for his own best interests but felt that he couldn't disappoint his distinguished patrons.

The first print completed was after Titian's *St. Peter Martyr* at the Dominican Church of Sts. Giovanni and Paolo. In coloring it is similar to the Rembrandt print, with gray-green sky, yellow lights, and cool brown shadows. While attractive and forceful, it is not as effective as the Rembrandt because Titian, with his greater range of color, presented a more complex problem. Most of the prints thereafter leaned to monochromes in either browns or greens. The *St. Peter* was finished in 1739 and in the same year five more prints were brought to completion.

In 1740 he produced the three sheets which made up Tintoretto's *Crucifixion* in the Scuola di San Rocco.[29] These were intended to be joined, if desired, to form one long print measuring about 22 x 50 inches.

Of the ten remaining subjects, the last, Jacopo Bassano's *Dives and Lazarus,* was finished at the end of 1743, and the set of 24 plates (some paintings, as noted, were reproduced in three sheets and some in two) was published as a bound volume by J. B. Pasquali in Venice, 1745, under the title *Titiani Vecelii, Pauli Caliarii, Jacobi Robusti et Jacobi de Ponte; opera selectiora a Joanne Baptista Jackson, Anglo, ligno coelata et coloribus adumbrata.*

---

[29] Jackson mentioned that he was seen drawing the blocks in the presence of Sir Roger Newdigate, Sir Bouchier Wrey "and other gentlemen of distinction." The reason for such reference was probably some comment that he might have traced his outlines from Agostino Carracci's 1582 engraving of the same subject in three large sheets (B. 23), each of which joins the others at precisely the same places as Jackson's sheets. I am indebted to Dr. Jakob Rosenberg of the Fogg Museum for pointing out these similarities.

The Venetian prints were not merely an extension of chiaroscuro, they represented a daring effort to go beyond line engraving for reproducing paintings. Justification for this attempt is given in the *Essay* (p. 6):

> ... and though those delicate Finishings, and minute Strokes, which make up great Part of the Merit of engraving on Copper, are not to be found in those cut on Wood in *Chiaro Oscuro;* yet there is a masterly and free Drawing, a boldness of Engraving and Relief, which pleases a true Taste more than all the little Exactness found in the Engravings on Copper Plates ... and indeed has an Effect which the best Judges very often prefer to any Prints from Engravings, done with all that Exactness, minute Strokes of the Graver, and Neatness of Work, which is sure to captivate the Minds of those whose Taste is formed upon the little Considerations of delicately handling the Tools, and not upon the Freedom, Life and Spirit of the separate Figures, and indeed the whole Composition.

A novel device, embossing, was employed to give added strength to the prints. This development had been foreshadowed by earlier prints and pages of text which showed a slight indentation where the dampened paper received the impression. Embossing had probably first been used systematically by Elisha Kirkall in 1722–24, and by Arthur Pond in his chiaroscuros, made in 1732–36 in conjunction with George Knapton, after drawings by old masters. Jackson admired Pond's work even though it combined etched outlines with two tone blocks printed from wood.[30] Pond's embossing was delicate and applied sparely only in certain forms, such as ruined columns, but Jackson's sunken areas were heavier and franker, consciously intended to give an all-over effect. Since the paper could not be pressed out without weakening the embossing, it often took on the scarred and buckled look that characterizes the Venetian chiaroscuros.

The set had occupied him for 4½ years, during which he had planned, cut, and proofed 94 blocks.

> No sooner was that ended, and a little Breathing required after that immense Fatigue, in the Year 1744 he attempted to print in Colours, and published six Landskips in Imitation of Painting in Acquarello.

---

[30] *Enquiry,* p. 35. The Japanese began to use embossing about 1730. See Reichel, 1926, p. 48.

TITLE PAGE for *Gajo Suetonio tranquillo, le vite de'dodici Cesari*, Piacentini, Venice, 1738.

This new set, dedicated to Robert d'Arcy, British Ambassador to the Republic of Venice, was based on gouache paintings by Marco Ricci, probably done on goatskin or leather in his usual manner. For Jackson to make these color prints was a logical step, since his work had tended toward the full chromatic range even in the chiaroscuros, which "adumbrated" color. His new prints were all color—clear, sensitive, and tonally just. It is not surprising that he seized upon Ricci's opaque watercolors. The paintings of the Venetian masters had darkened in ill-lit churches, the shadows had become murky, there were too many figures. But the Ricci paintings were small and clearly patterned, the color sparkled.

The original gouaches have not been located, but from other examples in the same manner, in Buckingham Palace and in the Uffizi, it is plain that Jackson took certain liberties. Ricci's rather sharp colors were considerably modified and mellowed when they weren't changed entirely: witness the two sets in different harmonies in the British Museum. Peter A. Wick (1955) believes it most likely that Jackson did not copy specific paintings, and suggests that details from Ricci's etchings and gouaches were combined and freely amended to create Ricci-like designs.

Having determined his color scheme Jackson cut seven to ten blocks, each designed to bear an individual color which was to combine with others when necessary to form new colors. No outline block was used. To obtain variations from light to dark in each pigment Jackson scraped down the blocks with a knife; he thus lowered the surfaces slightly and created porous textures which would introduce the white paper or the underlying color. Examination of the prints clearly shows granular textures in the light areas. Scraping to lighten impressions was a common procedure in black-and-white printmaking, and was described by both Papillon and Bewick. In addition Jackson no doubt used underlays, that is, small pieces of paper pasted in layers of diminishing size on the backs of the blocks where the color was most intense. The pressure was therefore greatest in the deepest notes and lightest in the scraped parts. The copper plate press enabled Jackson to get good register without making marks on the blocks. The paper was dampened and fastened to the chase at one end. After each impression the next inked block was slid into the chase and printed wet into wet. Problems of register were eliminated because the sheets were held in place at all times, the blocks fitting the same form. No doubt the paper was sprinkled with water on the reverse side after each impression to eliminate shrinking and to keep it soft for printing. This method would explain Jackson's transparent effects.

Although the Ricci prints were certainly the most ambitious and complexly planned prints of the century, the cutting is crisp and decisive and the effect fresh and unlabored. As in the Venetian set embossing is consciously applied. Most likely Jackson impressed the finished prints, specially redampened for the purpose, with one or two of the uninked blocks. Jackson interpreted Ricci's qualities with great spirit, and in doing so he liberated the color woodcut from its old conventions. The "true"-color prints he produced in the medium preceded the Japanese, if not the Chinese.[31] In Japan, it must be remembered, simple color printing in rose and green supplanted hand coloring in about 1741, and rudimentary polychrome prints can be dated as early as 1745, but, as Binyon[32] puts it, "it was not until 1764 that the first rather tentative *nishiki-ye,* or complete colour-prints were produced in Yedo, and the long reign of the Primitives came to an end."

In making his Ricci prints Jackson sought a method of color printing that would overcome the deficiencies of Jacob Christoph Le Blon's three-color mezzotint process. Le Blon, a Frenchman born in Germany, had begun experimenting with color printing as early as 1705. His idea was to split the chromatic components of a picture into three basic hues—blue, red, and yellow—in gradations of intensity so that varying amounts of color, each on a separate copper plate, could be printed in superimposition to reconstitute the original picture. This was based upon a simplification of Newton's seven primaries. Later, Le Blon added a fourth, black plate. Incredibly, this is the principle of modern commercial color printing, the only difference being that Le Blon did not have a camera, color filters, and the halftone screen at his disposal and had to make the separations by hand. Le Blon came to London in 1719, produced an enormous number of color prints, published his *Coloritto, or the Harmony of Colouring in Painting* in a very small edition about 1722 (it is undated), and shortly thereafter failed disastrously. About 1733 he returned to Paris, where he attracted a few followers. Most of his prints have disappeared, only about fifty being known at present.

---

[31] Altdorfer's *Beautiful Virgin of Ratisbon,* about 1520, (B. 51, vol. 8, p. 78) made use of five colors in some impressions (Lippmann describes one with seven colors) but these were used primarily for decorative, not naturalistic purposes.

[32] Laurence Binyon, *A Catalogue of Japanese & Chinese Woodcuts in the British Museum,* London, 1916, p. xx, introduction.

TRIAL PROOF of the key block of center sheet of *The Crucifixion,* after Tintoretto. National Gallery of Art (Rosenwald Collection).

TRIAL PROOF of the key block of *Christ on the Mount of Olives,* after Bassano. National Gallery of Art (Rosenwald Collection).

The idea of full-color printing, then, was in the air, although later, in the *Enquiry,* Jackson took pains to state that he had not been following in the footsteps of the Frenchman, who, he claimed, had made serious mistakes.

> The Curious may think that this Tentamine was taken from the celebrated Mr. *le Blond;* I must here take the Liberty to explain the Difference . . . Numbers are convinced already, that the printing Copper-plates done with *Fumo* or *Mezzotinto,* are the most subject to wear out the soonest of any sort of Engraving on that Metal. Had this one Article been properly considered, *le Blond,* must have seen the impossibility of printing any Quantity from his repeated Impressions of Blue, Red, and Yellow Plates, so as to produce only Twenty of these printed Pictures to be alike. This is obvious to every one who has any Knowledge, or has seen the cleaning of Copper-plates after the Colour was laid on; the delicate finishing of the Flesh must infallibly wear out every time the Plate is cleaned, and all the tender light Shadowing of any Colour must soon become white in proportion as the Plate wears. The Nature of Impression being overlooked at first, was the principal Cause that Undertaking came to nothing, notwithstanding the immense Expence the Proprietors were at to have a few imperfect Proofs at best, since it is evident they could be no other. The new invented Method of printing in Colours by Mr. *Jackson* is under no Apprehension of being wore out so soon . . . Whatever has been done by our *English* Artist, was all printed with Wood Blocks with a strong Relievo, and in Substance sufficient to draw off almost any number that may be required.

What Jackson neglected to mention was the difficulty of repeating transparent color effects with large planks of wood. Few existing impressions match each other and some prints are off register. What saved him was his fine color sense, his brilliance as a woodcutter, and his disinclination to make literal color reproductions.

The work that Jackson left behind became a part of the cultural heritage of Venice, valued on its own account as well as for its connection with the city. Zanetti[33] describes the Venetian set and Zanotto,[34] in his *Guida* of 1856, urges a visit to the Chiesa Abaziale della Misericordia, which evidently had on permanent exhibition a "perfectly unique collection of woodcuts in various colors by Jackson, quite unmatched."

---

[33] Zanetti, 1792, pp. 689, 716.   [34] Zanotto, 1856, p. 320, note 3.

Gallo[35] says that some of Jackson's blocks found their way to the printing house of the Remondini and were used to strike off new impressions, after which they became the property of the Typografia Pozzato in Bassano. This might explain some of the inferior examples of the Venetian set which could hardly have come from the presses of Jackson or Pasquali.

England Again: The Wallpaper Venture

JACKSON was married in Venice—whether to an Italian we do not know—and when he left the city in 1745 to return to England he took a family along. He mentions "an impoverish'd Family" in the *Essay,* but beyond this we know nothing of his personal life.

As soon as he arrived in England he was invited to work in a calico establishment, where he remained about six years. But making drawings to be printed on cloth failed to give him the scope he required. At the back of his mind was the passion to work with woodblocks in color. This led him to take a bold and hazardous step—to leave his position and attempt, obviously with little capital, the manufacture of wallpaper, not to please an established taste but to educate the public to a new type of product.

Wallpaper had come into popular use in England in the late 17th century, having been obtained from China by the East India Company. These hand-painted wall hangings, imported at great cost and in small quantities, were correspondingly expensive. The subjects were gay and fanciful—birds, fans, Chinese kiosks, pagodas, and flowers. Highly desired because they offered an escape from the heavy grandeur of the Baroque style, they were subsequently imitated by assembly-line methods. They fitted naturally into the developing *rocaille* style (corrupted into Rococo outside of France), and it is not surprising that they were also produced extensively in Paris. In England these imitations, which formed a substitute for expensive velvet and damask hangings, completely dominated the wallpaper field.

---

[35] Gallo, 1941, pp. 23–23. Jackson's blocks are not listed in the Remondini catalog of 1817.

The first notice of Jackson's venture appeared in the *Gentleman's Magazine* of February 1752.[36] A letter signed "Y. D." praised the editor "Sylvanus Urban" for attempting to revive the art of cutting on wood. It mentioned that this art was in decline for more than a century, but noted that—

> Two of our countrymen, *E. Kirkall* and *J. B. Jackson,* ought to be exempted from this general charge; the former having a few years ago introduced the *Chiaro Oscuro* of *Hugo de Carpi* into England, though he met with no extraordinary encouragement for his ingenuity; and the art had died with him had not the latter attempted to revive it, but with less encouragement than his predecessor. *Mr. Jackson,* however, has lately invented a new method of printing paper hangings from blocks, which is very ornamental, and exceeds the common method of paper-staining (as it is termed) by the delicacy of his drawings, the novelty of his designs, and the masterly arrangement of his principal figures.

The next notice appeared in the *London Evening Post* of April 30–May 2, 1752:

> New invented PAPER HANGINGS, printed in Oyl, which prevents the fading or changing of the Colours; as also Landscapes printed in Colours, by J. B. Jackson, Reviver of the Art of printing in Chiaro Oscuro, are to be had at Dunbar's Warehouse in Aldermanbury, London; or Mr. Gibson's, Bookseller, opposite the St. Alban's Tavern in Charles-street near St. James's-Square, and no where else.

Several months afterwards, in the September 1752 issue of *Gentleman's Magazine,* publication of the *Enquiry into the Origins of Printing in Europe* was announced.

The *Enquiry* is an odd book. It combines rewritten versions of two Jackson manuscripts, a study of the origins of printing in Europe and an autobiographical journal covering, we suppose, the years from about 1725 on. The writer, in his introduction, says that he had been attracted by the two notices mentioned and went to see Jackson, whom he already knew by reputation. As a "Lover of Art" he considered it his duty to acquaint the public with Jackson's ideas concerning the origins of printing. These ideas, he felt, were an important contribution. After devoting half the little book to a rambling account of this subject, including a short history of woodcutting from Dürer onward, the author suddenly shifts to the journal. It is regrettable that he condensed it because we do not know what was

---

[36] Vol. 22, pp. 77–79.

left out. It is possible that much autobiographical information was excluded, as well as a picture of woodcutters and woodcutting of the time. The book concludes with the statement that Jackson intended to print in October of that year (1752) a paper hanging in two sheets after an original painting "by *F. Simonnetta* of *Parma*"[37] representing the battle fought near that city in 1738.

This print was to be in full color, 3 feet 6 inches long by 2 feet high, and was to serve as a specimen for a series of four of the same size, the others being "History, Pictures and Landscapes." They were to be done by subscription:

> No Money will be required of the Subscribers till the Prints are finished, and only at the Delivery. It is to be hoped the Curious and the Public will encourage this Undertaking, by a Man who has spent the greatest Part of his Life in searching after and improving an Art, believed by all to be lost, and has restored it to the Condition we now see it in his Works.

The only known copy of this battle picture, made from about seven blocks, is in the Print Room of the British Museum. It is a magnificent piece. Probably nothing with this breadth of handling had ever been done in woodcut before. The color is grave and beautifully harmonized, although the paper has deteriorated and the colors have darkened somewhat. The blocks were cut with ardor, almost fury; everything is brought to life with masterly assurance. Martin Hardie, who made the only previous comment on this print, which he could only surmise was Jackson's, says:[38] "Jackson's supreme achievement is a large battle scene, with wonderful masses of rich colour superbly blended, reminiscent of Velasquez in breadth, in dignity, and in glory of tone."

There were competitors in London, among them Matthias Darley, who produced papers in the Chinese style; Thomas Bromwich, who was patronized by Walpole; and Robert Dunbar, Jr., of Aldermanbury, who in addition sold Jackson's papers. They lacked both Jackson's gifts and his unreasonable standards but they produced more generally acceptable wallpaper with greater facility. These competitors did not work in oil colors, like Jackson. Transparent tints were too difficult to control, especially when applied with inking balls (composition rollers

---

[37] There is little doubt that Jackson meant Francesco Simonini (1686–1753), a painter of battle subjects who was born in Parma and lived in Venice in the 1740's.

[38] Hardie, 1906, p. 23.

did not come into use until well after 1800), and effects were too heavy. They used distemper—powdered color mixed with glue and water, with chalk added to give body. This was sometimes applied with woodblock or stencil but most often it was simply painted in by hand over a blockprinted outline. Often the painting was done directly on the wall after the paper was hung. These wallpapers were weak when examined critically, but nobody worried as long as a light bright pastel effect was obtained. Jackson's vigorous drawing and woodcutting were out of place in this field. They were, like his tonal exactitude that made holes in the wall, a distraction and an offense against interior decoration.

Jackson's business, therefore, did not prosper. In a last effort to stir up public interest he published, in 1754, his well-known little book, *An Essay on the Invention of Engraving and Printing in Chiaro Oscuro,* illustrated with eight prints in "proper colours." It sold for two shillings and sixpence. The style was rather florid but his arguments were presented with such vigor that it is easy to see why critics have found it difficult to refrain from quoting at length. The main body of text is only eight pages long, with an additional eight pages of subsidiary descriptive material attached to the pictures.

On the title page appeared his favorite passage from Pascal, used previously on the title page of the *Enquiry:* "Ceux qui sont capables d'inventer sont rares: ceux qui n'inventent point sont en plus grand nombre, et par conséquent les plus forts." The first few pages of the *Essay* enlarge on this theme:

> It has been too generally the Fate of those who set themselves to the Inventing any Thing that requires Talents in the Discovery, to apply all their Faculties, exhaust their Fortune, and waste their whole Time in bringing that to Perfection, which when obtained, Age, Death, or Want of sufficient Supplies, obliges them to relinquish, and to yield all the Advantages which their Hopes had flattered them with, and which had supported their Spirits during their Fatigues and Difficulties, to others; and thus leave behind them an impoverish'd Family incapable to carry on their Parent's Design, and too often complaining of the projecting Genius of that Father who has ruin'd them, tho' he has enriched the Nation to which he belonged, and to which of Consequence he was a laudable Benefactor.

He proceeds in this bitter vein for a time, then brings into the open the main purpose of the book:

> Another Reason perhaps is, that the Artist being totally engaged in the Pursuit of his Discovery, has but little Time to apply to the Lovers and Encouragers of Art for their Patronage, Protection, and Supplies necessary for the carrying on such a Design, or he has not Powers to set the Advantage which would result from it in a true Light; nor communicate in Words what he clearly conceived in Idea: for certainly there are Men enough, who from the mere Desire of increasing their Wealth, would give him that Assistance, which, like the artificial Heat of a Greenhouse, would bring that Art to a Ripeness, which would otherwise languish and die under the Coldness of the first Designer, and which in this Union of Riches and Invention would yield mutual Advantage to both.
>
> There are besides this amongst the Great, without Doubt, many who would gladly lend their Patronage to rising Arts, if they knew their Authors. . . .

He gives as example the Duke of Cumberland, who had just sponsored a tapestry plant at Fulham, and follows with an outline of the honorable traditions of the woodcut, pointing out that Dürer, Titian, Salviati, Campagnola, and other painters drew their work on woodblocks to be cut by woodcutters, and adds that "even *Andrea Vincentino* did not think it in the least a Dishonour, though a Painter, to grave on Wood the Landscapes of *Titian*." He builds up to the statement that Raphael and Parmigianino drew on woodblocks to be cut in chiaroscuro by Ugo da Carpi.

> After having said all this, it may seem highly improper to give to Mr. *Jackson* [he speaks of himself throughout in the third person] the Merit of inventing this Art; but let me be permitted to say, that an Art recovered is little less than an Art invented. The Works of the former Artists remain indeed; but the Manner in which they were done, is entirely lost: the inventing then the Manner is really due to this latter Undertaker, since no Writings, or other Remains, are to be found by which the Method of former Artists can be discover'd, or in what Manner they executed their works; nor, in Truth, has the *Italian* Method since the Beginning of the 16th Century been attempted by any one except Mr. *Jackson*.

We cannot help concluding that Jackson was falsifying here. Taking advantage of the public's ignorance, he was puffing up his historical importance in order to sell wallpaper. If the *cognoscenti* complained that he had buried the chiaroscurists after da Carpi, he always had the explanation that others did not work in the Italian style, which he neglected to describe. Jackson knew what he was doing; he was not as ignorant of art history as Hardie and Burch have surmised, although it is true that he was not always certain as to dates, since he believed Andreani worked as a contemporary of da Carpi. In the *Enquiry,* published only two years earlier, he had shown familiarity with the prints of Goltzius, Coriolano, Businck, Nicolas and Vincent Le Sueur, Moretti, and Zanetti, all of whom had worked to some extent in the Italian manner.

Some writers have reacted strongly to this paragraph. Losing their sense of proportion, they have been led to the conclusion that Jackson was little better than a charlatan and that his work as a whole reflected his low ethics. In some instances his culpability has been magnified: Bénézit has even charged him with claiming to have invented color printing.

The worst result of Jackson's insistence on re-inventing the Italian manner was that it made a major issue of what was at best a minor honor. It minimized such technical contributions as the following, which did not follow traditional recipes:

> . . . Mr. *Jackson* has invented ten positive Tints in *Chiaro Oscuro;* whereas Hugo di Carpi knew but four; all of which can be taken off by four Impressions only.

This technical system was used for the Venetian chiaroscuros, the portrait of Algernon Sidney after Justus Verus, and others. He did not mention that he needed a greater range of tones because he was working after oil paintings, not drawings. The introduction of full color from a series of blocks to translate water colors is also mentioned in the *Essay,* but with no greater emphasis than in the *Enquiry.* Since his wallpaper was to be done in color as well as in chiaroscuro, and since the *Essay* included four plates in color, it is astonishing that Jackson failed to make stronger claims for his originality in this development.

He proceeded to describe his plan to replace wallpapers in the Chinese style with his papers, which, he stated, would have no ". . . gay glaring Colours in broad Patches of red, green, yellow, blue &c . . . [with] no true Judgment belonging to it . . . Nor are there Lions leaping from Bough to Bough like Cats, Houses in the Air, Clouds and Sky upon the Ground . . . ."

He proposed, instead, to use as subjects many of the famous statues of antiquity; the landscapes of Salvator Rosa, Claude Lorrain, Poussin, Berghem, Wouwerman, the views of Canaletto, Pannini—

> Copies of the Pictures of all the best Painters of the *Italian, French* and *Flemish* Schools, the fine sculptur'd Vases of the Ancients which are now remaining; in short, every Bird that flies, every Figure that moves upon the Surface of the Earth from the Insect to the human; and every Vegetable that springs from the Ground, whatever is of Art or Nature, may be introduced into this Design of fitting up and furnishing Rooms, with all the Truth of Drawing, Light, and Shadow, and great Perfection of Colouring.

This vast gallery of art and nature was to be printed in "Colours softening into each other, with Harmony and Repose . . . ."

Even if we feel that Jackson was building up his project to attract attention, or that he was intoxicated by the idea of creating art on such a grand scale, there is still something wrong in his conceiving it in terms of wallpaper. What is certain is that Jackson was desperately anxious to create color prints. In the absence of art patrons, wallpaper was his only excuse for continuing as an artist. As a business venture it was absurd, even tragic. There is good reason to believe that Jackson lacked capital and rented the quarters for his business: his name does not appear in the Poor Rate Book of that period in the Borough of Battersea.

From a certain standpoint, this excursion by Jackson into wallpapers featuring Roman ruins and classical antiquity appeared to come at an appropriate time. Marco Ricci's paintings as well as the somewhat later work of Pannini and Zuccarelli, and Guardi's early ruin pieces, were already known. Ricci had visited England from 1710 to 1716. Zuccarelli had come twice, once in 1742 and again in 1751 to stay until 1773, becoming a foundation member of the Royal Academy; his classical landscapes with their glib charm had a comparatively good reception. But the strongest influence was undoubtedly that of Piranesi, whose powerful etchings brought to life as never before the ravaged stones of Imperial Rome and the *Campagna*. Their effect was widespread and electrifying, although it was not until the 1760's that they developed their full force as an influence on English architecture and furniture design, and came to supersede the Palladian style brought to England by Inigo Jones at the beginning of the 17th century.

Jackson was too early; public taste was not yet ready for picturesque landscape or antique forms in wallpaper. But the style became dominant in the latter 18th century, particularly in England and France, and was also exported to America. While it is difficult to estimate the degree of Jackson's influence in this development, we know that no scenic papers can be dated before the Ricci prints, or before Jackson's wallpaper venture. Oman[39] comments:

> The use of wall-paper to imitate large architectural designs dates, as we have seen, from the days of J. B. Jackson. During the remainder of the century this style was used almost exclusively for decoration of the halls and staircases of great houses.

These papers covered rooms with landscape panoramas or with landscapes in Rococo scroll frames, relieved by decorative panels with busts, statuettes, and floral ornaments. As in preceding work, they were usually painted in opaque water colors. Most of the landscapes were loose transcriptions of designs by Pannini, Vernet, Lancret and other painters of architectural, scenic, and pastoral subjects. The treatment was generalized and superficial, the touch light and detached.

In this approach to wallpaper we see the basic ideas of Jackson, but with more emphasis on charm and elegance. Ironically, as years passed and original sources grew obscure, it became the tendency to attribute scenic papers in great houses to Jackson.[40] If he was a failure as a pioneer in the field, he remained its most highly prized legend.

The *Essay* continued with a criticism of the current taste in wallpaper. Jackson enlarged on the lack of discrimination of persons who would prefer popular papers to his.

> It seems, also, as if there was great Reason to suspect wherever one sees such preposterous Furniture, that the Taste in Literature of that Person who directed it was very deficient, and that it would prefer *Tom D'Urfy* to *Shakespear, Sir Richard Blackmore* to *Milton, Tate* to *Homer,* an *Anagrammatist* to *Virgil, Horace,* or any other Writer of true Wit, either Ancient or Modern.

He added that his prints, made in oil colors, would be permanent "whereas in that done with Water-Colours, in the common Way, Six Months makes a very visible Alteration in all that preposterous Glare, which makes its whole Merit. . . ."

The *Essay* has eight plates, four of ancient statues in chiaroscuro and four of plants, animals, and buildings, in probably six colors. They were hastily done and no doubt had a rather fresh charm when published, but unfortunately the oil in the pigments was inferior, and every print in the book has darkened and yellowed

---

[39] Oman, 1929, p. 33.
[40] An excellent description of the papers of this type imported to America is given by Edna Donnell in *Metropolitan Museum Studies* 1932, vol. 4, pp. 77–108.

badly. The prints and neighboring pages are heavily spotted and stained. This book which should have been his vindication became instead an argument for his lack of merit, especially to those who were not familiar with his other work.

We do not know how large a working force Jackson had or how many of the projected plates he planned to assign to helpers or to carry out himself. Some of the decorative borders from four blocks, blue, red, yellow, and gray-green, he undoubtedly made and printed himself. They are heavy and rather fruity in effect but are incisively drawn and cut. Also bearing Jackson's stamp are some ornamental frames with fruit and flowers in the same full range of colors.

An album ascribed to him, in the collection of the Victoria and Albert Museum, contains drawings of flowers, foliage, details of ornament and hand-colored designs, and a proof of the woodcut for the title page to the *Suetonius* of 1738. Five of the drawings are signed or initialed by Jackson, with dates from 1740 to 1753. The designs, which might have been intended for calico or wallpaper, are poorly done and not at all in his style. The drawings are competent but cannot definitely be considered his, notwithstanding the signatures, since we do not know Jackson's handwriting from other sources. The most that can be said for this album is that it probably comes from his workshop.

While producing wallpaper, Jackson still made efforts to attract sponsors for full editions of his earlier chiaroscuros. The *Woman Meditating* was dedicated to the Antiquarian Society of London. *Christ Giving the Keys to St. Peter,* rejected by Crozat, we assume, was dedicated to Thomas Hollis, whom Jackson may have met in Venice. And the *Venus and Cupid with a Bow* was inscribed to Thomas Brand, lifelong companion of Hollis who later added to his name the latter's patronymic. The *Algernon Sidney* has no dedication, but since Hollis was a Sidney specialist and edited the first one-volume edition of his works in 1769, there is a strong likelihood that the print had some connection with this liberal gentleman. Jackson made it either in Venice just before he left, or in England shortly after his arrival.

Robert Dunbar, Jr., who had inherited the wallpaper manufactory on his father's death, went out of business late in 1754. In his possession was a quantity of Jackson's papers, for which he was the main outlet. With this backlog of papers on hand, and no large distributor, Jackson's venture collapsed. This happened shortly after the publication of the *Essay,* and its author was never to have the opportunity to carry out his grandiose plans.

Jackson appealed to Hollis, who wrote to his former mentor, Dr. John Ward, professor of rhetoric at Gresham College and the head of a society founded by noblemen and gentlemen for the encouragement of learning:[41]

> Dear Sir!—Do Me the Favour to accept these four prints of Jackson's. They are no where sold, & will soon be scarce. When You consider their Merit, I am confident You will lament the hard Fate of the ingenious Artist; who, at this Time, in his old age, & in his own Country is unprotected unnoticed, and can difficultly support Himself against immediate distress & Ruin.
> I am, with great Respect,
> Dear Sir!
>
> Your obliged affect humble Servant
> T. Hollis
>
> Bedford Street, February 10, 1755

We do not know the results of this appeal. In any case Jackson seems to have faded out as an artist. Little is known of his subsequent career up to the time more than twenty years later, when Bewick mentions meeting him in advanced age. In 1761 he made a drawing of Salisbury Cathedral for Edward Eaton, "bookseller at Sarum," for a line engraving dedicated by Eaton to the Lord Bishop of Winchester. This large view included figures in the foreground in an attempt to give animation to the scene. Unfortunately the engraver, John Fougeron, was little more than an amateur. His execution was feeble and mechanical: Jackson's drawing suffered so badly that its quality cannot be determined. This print was copied on a smaller scale in a steel engraving by J. B. Swaine, published by J. B. Nichols & Son in 1843, but it was hardly an improvement.

Bewick's recollections of Jackson, written about forty years after their meeting in Newcastle, imply that Jackson stayed in that city for a period. The Town Clerk's Office, however, has no record of his residence. The following passage from Bewick's *Memoir* is the last evidence [42] bearing on Jackson:

> Several impressions from duplicate or triplicate blocks, printed in this way, of a very large size, were also given to me, as well as a drawing of the press from

---

[41] British Museum Add. mss. 6210.   [42] Bewick, 1925, pp. 213–214.

which they were printed, many years ago, by Jean Baptiste Jackson, who had been patronised by the King of France; but, whether these prints had been done with the design of embellishing the walls of houses in that country, I know not. They had been taken from paintings of eminent old masters, and were mostly Scripture pieces. They were well drawn, and perhaps correctly copied from the originals, yet in my opinion none of them looked well. Jackson left Newcastle quite enfeebled with age, and, it was said, ended his days in an asylum, under the protecting care of Sir Gilbert Elliot, Bart., at some place on the border near the Teviot, or on Tweedside.

If Bewick was correct in reporting that Jackson died while under the protection of Sir Gilbert Elliot, probably in a Poor Law institution, it is unlikely that the date could have been much later than 1777, the year in which Sir Gilbert died. This would place the meeting of both artists shortly before this time, when Bewick was in his early twenties (he was born in 1753). Sir Gilbert lived in Minto House, Roxburghshire, Scotland, but no evidence can be found for the supposition that Jackson died in the vicinity. No obituary has been discovered. The record of Jackson's death, if it exists, probably lies in a parish register somewhere on the Scottish border.

Critical Opinion

IN MOST histories of prints it was considered sufficient to note that certain artists worked in woodcut chiaroscuro; the quality of such work was rarely discussed. But Jackson was an exception: something about his prints aroused critics to defense or attack. The cleavage is absolute, strange for one who was presumably a mere reproductive artist. Nothing could show more clearly the unsettled nature of Jackson's standing than a sampling of these opinions.

Horace Walpole in a letter, dated June 12, 1753, to Sir Horace Mann describing the furnishings in Strawberry Hill, commented:[43]

> The bow window below leads into a little parlour hung with a stone-colour Gothic paper and Jackson's Venetian prints, which I could never endure while they pretended, infamous as they are, to be after Titian, &c., but when I gave them this air of barbarous bas-reliefs, they succeeded to a miracle; it is impossible at first sight not to conclude that they contain the history of Attila or Tottila done about the very era.

Von Heinecken[44] says they are "in the manner of Hugo da Carpi but much inferior in execution." But Huber, Rost, and Martini[45] noted Jackson's independent approach:

> Jackson's prints, which are certainly not without merit, are in general less sought after by collectors than they deserve. His style is original and is concerned entirely with broad effects.

Baverel[46] also had a high opinion of Jackson's work. Describing the Venetian prints, he says that Jackson "had a skillful and daring attack, and it is regrettable that he did not produce more work." Nagler's[47] criticism typifies the academic preconceptions of some writers on the subject of chiaroscuro:

---

[43] *The Letters of Horace Walpole,* ed. Toynbee, 1903, vol. 3, p. 166.
[44] Von Heinecken, 1771, p. 94.
[45] Huber, Rost, and Martini, 1808, vol. 9, pp. 121–123.
[46] Baverel, 1807, vol. 1, pp. 341–342.
[47] Künstler-Lexicon, op. cit.

Jackson's works are not praiseworthy throughout in drawing, and also he was not thoroughly able to apply the principles of chiaroscuro correctly. . . . Yet we have several valuable prints from Jackson. . . .

And Chatto [48] remarks:

> They are very unequal in point of merit; some of them appearing harsh and crude, and others flat and spiritless, when compared with similar products by the old Italian wood engravers.

With this verdict W. J. Linton [49] disagrees, saying, ". . . Chatto underrates him. I find his works very excellent and effective. *The Finding of Moses* (2 feet high by 16 inches wide) and *Virgin Climbing the Steps of the Temple* (after Veronese), and others, are admirable in every respect . . . ." Duplessis [50] attacks the Venetian set heatedly and at length, yet he devotes more space to expounding Jackson's deficiencies than to discussing the work of any other woodcut artist, even Dürer or da Carpi.

On the evidence we have, the new conception Jackson brought to printmaking was not fully understood until the 20th century. Pierre Gusman [51] in 1916 probably first noted the technical distinction between Jackson's work and earlier chiaroscuros.

> He [Jackson] conceived his prints in a different way from the Italians, bringing in new aspects in accenting values and planes, because he did not reproduce drawings but interpreted paintings. The whites even show embossings in the paper to make the light vibrate, and a specially cut block is sometimes impressed to help in modeling the forms. Jackson, in short, very much the wood carver, combined the resources of the cameo with those of the chiaroscuro and produced curious works of combined techniques, but without equaling his predecessors, who were particularly remarkable for their simplicity of style and treatment.

---

[48] Chatto and Jackson, 1861, p. 455.

[49] Linton, 1889, p. 214. The second print mentioned is after Titian, not Veronese.

[50] Duplessis, 1880, pp. 314–315. Duplessis, who was *conservateur-adjoint* in the Cabinet des Estampes of the Bibliothèque Nationale, no doubt based his judgment on the impressions in that collection. Certainly few of these were printed by either Jackson or Pasquali.

[51] Gusman, 1916, pp. 164, 165.

One year later, in 1917, Max J. Friedländer [52] commented that relief effects in block printing were not alien additions but natural consequences of the method. His main emphasis, we note, is on the Ricci prints.

> A peculiarity of the color woodcut, which first was put up with as a characteristic of the technique but finally was enhanced and utilized fully as a means of expression, is the physical relief that stands out in thick and soft paper with the sharp pressure of the wood-blocks. . . . No one has employed the relief of the woodcut so consciously and artfully as the Englishman John Baptist Jackson in the eighteenth century, who, particularly in some landscapes, created most effective and richly colored sheets. He has gone so far as to express forms in "blind-printing," entirely without bordering lines or contrasting colors, merely through relief pressing.

Anton Reichel's important history of chiaroscuro, with its magnificent color plates in facsimile, appeared in 1926.[53] He says of Jackson that his activity in chiaroscuro was "extraordinarily rich," that he created broad approximations of his subjects which made him neglect details, but that these were "convincingly translated into the language of the woodcut."

> Five heroic landscapes after M. Ricci represent the artistic high point of his work, having a distinctive richness of color not previously attained by any other master of chiaroscuro. Each of the prints has a complete harmony of colors; the single color blocks—over ten can be counted in each print—which show in their separate tones the extraordinarily cultivated taste of the artist, give the composition a decorative effect far from any realistic imitation of nature. . . . The relief impressed with the blocks is so strong that, going beyond all other prior attempts of the kind, it represents an essential factor of the composition through its actual light-and-shadow effects.

Although by this time Jackson's chiaroscuros were regarded with respect and his color prints were acknowledged to be of prime importance, some of the conservative wallpaper historians were still repelled by their vigor, which did not suit genteel notions of interior decoration. Sugden and Edmondson [54] in 1925 cer-

---

[52] Friedländer, 1926 (1st ed. 1917), pp. 224–226.
[53] Reichel, 1926, p. 48.
[54] Sugden and Edmondson, 1925, p. 71.

tainly failed to understand both Jackson's work and the period in which it was done. They comment:

> Jackson's bold claims to originality and merit are scarcely borne out by anything he is known to have achieved. That he had a vogue, however, seems certain, for apart from his "Essay" he has come down to us as a historical figure. To modern tastes in art many of his productions seem almost monstrous, and yet they were to some extent the expression of the time-spirit in which they were born.

Postscript

WHILE Jackson had an influence on a small coterie, it did not prolong the life of the color woodcut. In Europe the medium did not survive his disappearance in 1755; no doubt it seemed to later artists intractable and lacking in nuance. The black-and-white woodcut, moreover, went into further decline and was almost entirely disregarded except for the rudest sort of work. Almost a century and a half were to pass before Gauguin and Munch swept aside old taboos and found exciting new possibilities for color in the woodcut process.

The lack of interest in the color woodcut was also the result of new techniques in the copper-plate media, techniques that could be adapted to color printing. In 1756 J. C. François introduced the crayon manner, an etching process that could imitate the effects of chalk and crayon drawings. During the following decades numerous technical variations were developed, the most popular being the pastel manner, the stipple, and the aquatint.

Of these methods only aquatint survived after early years of the 19th century. It was less limited than its companion processes and had wide application in rendering the effect of water-color wash. But color work in this medium, however attractive to a public that appreciated delicacy and charm, did not have mass appeal. The new audience created by the advancing Industrial Revolution wanted printed pictures of a less subtle type; they preferred imitations of sentimental,

THO. HOLLIS *Arm.* Hospic. Lincoln.   D. D. D.   J. B. Jackson *sculptor.*

1. Christ Giving the Keys to St. Peter, after Raphael

2. VENUS AND CUPID WITH A BOW, after Parmigianino

5. WOMAN MEDITATING (ST. THAIS?), after etching by Parmigianino

13. DESCENT FROM THE CROSS, after Rembrandt

43. HEROIC LANDSCAPE WITH WATERING PLACE, RIDERS, AND OBELISK, after Marco Ricci

40. HEROIC LANDSCAPE WITH FISHERMAN, COWS, AND HORSEMEN, after Marco Ricci

40. Heroic Landscape with Fisherman, Cows, and Horsemen, after Marco Ricci, Detail

49. Ornamental Frame with Flowers and Girl's Head
59. Woman Standing Holding Apron

53. BUILDING AND VEGETABLE

22. THE CRUCIFIXION, after Tintoretto, center sheet

22. THE CRUCIFIXION, after Tintoretto, left sheet

22. THE CRUCIFIXION, after Tintoretto, right sheet

banal, story-telling oil paintings with a high, waxy finish. Neither aquatint nor other copper-plate media were suitable for these products, and color lithography did not receive serious attention until the late 1830's. The wood engraving, which had inherited the function of the woodcut and which had greater flexibility in rendering tones and details, became the logical vehicle for the new color picture.

In this situation Jackson suddenly appeared as the pioneer, as the father of printed pictures based upon paintings in oil or water colors. His intention had been translation rather than imitation and he would have abhorred the feeble new product, but this did not concern his successors—they were interested only in his technical principles. Moreover, in their naïveté, they imagined they were improving on Jackson because their prints were counterfeit paintings while his were not.

The earliest picture printers therefore, used wood engraving. Among them were Frederich W. Gubitz of Berlin, who began the revival about 1815; William Savage[55] of London, a printer who published a book describing his project in 1822; and George Baxter of London, whose work dates from about 1830. All started with chiaroscuro and moved to full color from a large number of wood blocks, although in 1836 Baxter began printing his transparent oil colors over a base of steel engraving reinforced with aquatint. Only Baxter persevered and was rewarded by sensational popular success. His glassy and trivial prints with their high sweet finish enjoyed a vogue among collectors that lasted into the 20th century. In about 1860, however, he was driven from the market by the rise of a cheaper medium, chromolithography, which was responsible in the next few decades for a universal outpouring of popular bathos. This was picture printing in color geared for the mass audience.

It may seem an anticlimax to trace the color woodcut from Jackson to Baxter, and finally to chromolithography, but it is not irrelevant. Although spurned by the better artists, color had too popular an appeal to be ignored. It was inescapable that Jackson's successful technical procedures should finally be adopted and corrupted in the area of commerce.

Woodcut artists up to Jackson, with few exceptions, had used color for one major purpose, to reproduce drawings in line and tone. By enlarging the conception of the color woodcut Jackson brought the primitive chiaroscuro phase of its

---

[55] Savage, 1822. Jackson's pioneer work is acknowledged, pp. 15–16.

history to an end. After him, the chiaroscuro could not be practiced again except as an archaism.[56] The way was open for the modern woodcut, although it was a long time in coming.

The range of Jackson's work in tone and color exceeded that of all previous woodcutters and can be divided as follows: (1) chiaroscuros—after drawings, after paintings, after his own pen and ink drawings after paintings, interpretations of engravings and etchings, and interpretations of sculpture; and (2) full color—after paintings in gouache and after his own water colors. In addition he treated pictorial subjects in flat color areas without a key or outline block, a procedure used before him only by the 17th-century Chinese; and he combined burin work with knife cutting.

But Jackson's reputation, in the long perspective, must rest upon his qualities as an artist. He had great distinction as a colorist but lacked originality as a designer and was dependent upon others, for the most part, for basic compositions. As an interpreter of these compositions, however, he was imaginative and forceful. He did not follow the example of most copper plate engravers and reproduce subjects faithfully; his conception of the woodcut as a frank medium precluded exact rendition. Except, possibly, for his first chiaroscuro, he always translated freely, with the aim of making good woodcuts rather than accurate representations of his subjects. Jackson's work after others, in short, was consciously intended as artful approximation. This emphasis on the spirit rather than the letter, together with his novel techniques, often gave his prints a somewhat hybrid character—an ambiguous look that might serve to explain the uneasy feelings of many critics. But his largeness of feeling is unmistakable, and this is what finally places him among the masters.

The color woodcut is now an important form of printmaking. For this medium in the Western world, Jackson is the main ancestral figure.

---

[56] Only one moderately important chiaroscurist can be mentioned, John Skippe, who worked in England from the 1770's to about 1810.

CATALOG

JACKSON'S chiaroscuros and color woodcuts have been grouped under three headings. The first and main section includes, besides those of unquestionable authenticity, prints which can be attributed to Jackson with some degree of certainty and those actually seen by earlier writers but which have apparently disappeared. In each case the status of the print in Jackson's *oeuvre* has been noted.

The second section lists pieces believed to be by Jackson's workshop. Prints that might have been done independently by close followers have been included here because we have no evidence that would permit distinctions to be drawn.

The last section lists unverified subjects attributed to Jackson in a number of museums but which have been lost through war or other causes, and doubtful titles found in Nagler and Le Blanc. In each category the prints have been listed in chronological order as far as this can be determined. The sequence of the Venetian set follows Jackson's description in the *Enquiry,* although the prints themselves are dated somewhat differently.

One difficulty in cataloging Jackson's work is the prevailing confusion in titling, the same prints being listed differently in different collections. This was to be expected since the artist almost invariably omitted titles. Nagler's and Le Blanc's catalogs are not descriptive and consequently there has been much guesswork in checking titles, particularly since the Venetian set and the Ricci prints are only partially listed by both writers, and not entirely correctly. Where subjects have not been recorded at all, the variation in titling has been greater.

The location of prints has been given, with the exception of those in the Venetian set and in the *Essay,* which are, in part or whole, in too many collections to make listing feasible. It is not to be taken as complete. Jackson prints in a number of museums, particularly in Germany, have disappeared but might turn up again; some are still packed in boxes and await return to collections. For the sake of simplicity the names of cities alone have been used with the understanding that the chief print collection is meant. Exceptions are Boston where the Museum of Fine Arts is abbreviated to MFA and the Fogg Art Museum is shortened to Fogg, New York where the Metropolitan Museum of Art is listed as MMA and the New York Public Library as NYPL, and London where the British Museum is noted as BM and the Victoria & Albert as V & A.

The woodcuts reproduced are numbered according to this catalog, and placed as nearly as possible in the same order. When prints have been listed by Nagler or Le Blanc their corresponding numbers have been included. Print sizes are given in inches, vertical sides first.

Prints by Jackson

1.

Christ Giving the Keys to St. Peter, after Raphael [Le Bl. 7, N. 9]
    Dimensions:
7¼ x 9¾ inches with letters, 6½ x 9¾ inches without letters.
    Blocks, 4:
Light brown, light gray-brown, gray-brown, black.
    Inscription, lower left:
"*Raph. Urb. inv.*"
    Below, under border:
"Tho. Hollis *Arm*. Hospit. Lincoln. D. D. D. J. B. Jackſon *sculptor*."
About 1727. The dedication was added about 1750. After a drawing, now in the Louvre, for Raphael's tapestry cartoons.

                                                                     MFA, BM, Berlin-Dahlem

2.

Venus and Cupid with a Bow, after Parmigianino
    Dimensions:
9¾ x 6¼ inches with letters, 8¾ x 6¼ inches without letters.
    Blocks, 4:
Buff, light brown, terra-cotta red, black.
    Inscription, bottom:
"Tho. Brand *Arm*. Hospit. Temp. D. D. D./J. B. Jackſon *sculptor*."
    Left, running vertically:
"*F. M. Parm. inv.*"
1731.

The dedication was added about 1750. Other impressions occur in a combination of green and brown and also in gray and green. Five impressions are in the British Museum including one in which two slanting vertical lines in the table immediately to the left of Cupid's left leg are omitted.

Philadelphia, MFA, BM, V&A, Berlin-Dahlem, Rotterdam, Brussels

3.

Woman Standing Holding Jar on Her Head, after Parmigianino
  Dimensions:
    6¾ x 3½ inches.
  Blocks, 2:
    Mustard yellow, black.
  Inscription, at bottom:
    "*Per Illustri, ac Præclaro Viro* JOSEPH SMITH/*J. B. Jackson Humiliter Dedicat Donat, et*/*Sculpsit.* 1731."
  Another state has the following added in small letters:
    "Antonius Ma Zanetti a Jacobo Parmense Delin."
  The block for the tone is in two versions. The one illustrated is dotted in the jar to show gradations, while the other one is more loosely handled.
  Free copy of line engraving by G. A. Faldoni.

BM, V&A

4.

Headpiece with Landscape and Ruins
  This print is listed in the Staatliche Kunstsammlungen, Dresden, but has been lost in the war. No information as to color or size is available. The card catalogue has the following description:
    "Ruins to the left. In the middle going over a river is a bridge. To the right is a city view with campanile, dome and other buildings. Dated 1731."
  Probably made for use in a book. This seems to be the print described by Baverel and the "*petite vue*" Papillon mentioned.

5.

Woman Meditating (St. Thais?), after Parmigianino
  Dimensions:
    15⅜ x 9¼ inches with letters, 10¾ x 9¼ inches without letters.
  Blocks, 2: Pale brown, black. Also in green and blue-green.
    After etching by Parmigianino (B. 10).

Inscription, left near top, running diagonally upward:
"*F: M: Parmenˢ /Inventor/J: B: Jackſon Del/Sculp & excudit.*"

Bottom, beneath lower border:

"Societati Antiquariæ Londinensi/*Humillime* D.D.D. J.B.J

*Certo da cor, ch'alto deſtin non Scelſe,
Son l'impreſe magnanime neglette;
Ma le bell'alme alle bell'opre elette
Sanno gioir nelle fatiche eccelſe;
Nè biaſmo popolar, frale catena,
Spirto d'onore, il ſuo cammin raffrena.*"

This inscription was added much later, about 1750.

MFA, MMA, Philadelphia
BM, Berlin-Dahlem, Vienna, Bremen, Brussels, Amsterdam, Dresden

6.

Ulysses and Polyphemus, after Primaticcio

Dimensions:

7¾ x 10⅛ inches.

Blocks, 2:

Greenish yellow, black.

Inscription, bottom right:

"J. 9"

Some copies lack the inscription. This is from plate 9 of Theodor Van Thulden's 58 etchings reproducing designs by Primaticcio in Fontainebleau, published as "*Les Travaux d'Ulisse*" by P. Mariette in Paris, 1633.

These etchings were published again in 1740 as "*Errores Ulyssis.*" Listed as by Jackson in Weigel's *Kunstlagercatalog,* 1843, vol. 2, p. 103.

BM, V&A

7.

Bookplate

Dimensions:

4¼ x 6 inches, approximately.

Blocks, 2:

Reddish brown, black.

Inscription left and right top, in ribbon:

"Litterarum Felicitas"

BM

8.

Judgment of Solomon, after Rubens

 Dimensions:

  17 x 20⅜ inches.

 Blocks, 4:

  Yellow-buff, light brown, violet-brown, dark brown.

 Inscription, lower right:

  "Ill.*mo* et Exc.*mo* D.D. PHILIPPO FARSETTI,/*Patritio* VENETO, *Patrono suo* Benefic.*mo*/Tabulam *hanc* PETRI PAULI RUBENS./*In Ligno cœlavit, et in sui Obsequii et grati Animi*/Monumentum *humiliter Devovet J. B. Jackson.*"

 1735.

BM, Brussels, Venice

9.

The Visitation, after Annibale Carracci

 Dimensions:

  14¼ x 10¼ inches.

 Blocks, 4:

  Light yellow, buff, brown, dark gray.

 Inscription, upper right:

  "*A. Caratius Pinx*.*/J: B: Jackson Fecit*/VENEZIA 1735."

 Weigel described this print as *Der Besuch bei Elisabeth* in his *Kunstlagercatalog,* 1843, vol. 2, p. 103.

Smithsonian Institution (U.S. National Museum)
MFA, Philadelphia, BM, Dresden

10.

Julius Caesar, after Titian

 Dimensions:

  12 x 9½ inches.

 Blocks, 4:

  Tones of brown with dark brown key block.

 About 1738.

 This is a free translation of an engraving by Egidius Sadeler [Le Bl. 143] after one of a series of Roman emperors attributed to Titian. The original paintings have been lost.

BM

11.

St. Rocco, after Cherubino Alberti

Dimensions:

12¼ x 10¼ inches.

Blocks, 3:

Green, reddish tan, black.

"S. Rocco" added by another hand.

Some impressions lack the inscription. Also in two colors, mustard yellow and black.

Free transcription of a line engraving by Cherubino Alberti after an undetermined painter (Le Bl. 61). A facsimile in grayed chartreuse and black was published by the Reichsdruckerei in Berlin, about 1925.

MFA, BM

12.

Statuette of Neptune, after Giovanni da Bologna [Le Bl. 19, N. 8]

Dimensions:

22½ x 15⅜ inches.

Blocks, 4:

Tones of tan and brown.

Inscription, bottom:

"*Ex Prototypo Æreo* JOANNIS· BOLONIA *Duacensis in/Museo* D: JOSEPHI SMITH *Venetiis./J. B. Jackſon Anglus Sculp & exc.*"

About 1738.

The first state is without letters. Third state has inscription on top of statue base, "GUL. LLOYD *Arm. D.D.D. J.B.J.*"

Smithsonian Institution (U.S. National Museum)

MFA, Los Angeles, BM, Paris, Berlin-Dahlem, Wiemar, Amsterdam

13.

Descent from the Cross, after Rembrandt [Le Bl. 10, N. 3]

Dimensions:

14 x 11 inches (arched print).

Blocks, 4:

Yellow, gray, light brown, dark violet-brown.

Inscription, bottom left:

"*Rembrandt pinxit, alt. p. 1. lat. unc x. Extat Venetiis in domo* J: SMITH."

Bottom right:

"*J: B: Jackson figuras juxta Archetypum Sculp. & excudit. 1738.*"

Bottom:
"Accepterunt ergo Corpus JESU, & ligaverunt illud linteis/cum Aromatibus, ficut mos eft Judæis fepelire. *S.Joan. Cap.* XIX *Ver.* XI."/
Lower, with coat of arms:
"*Perillustri ac Praeclaro* VIRO D. JOSEPHO *Smith/Insigne hoc Opus affabre in Ligno coelavit, & in sui/obseqii & grati Animi monu-mentum humiliter devovet/J: B: Jackson*"

         Smithsonian Institution (U.S. National Museum)
      MFA, Fogg, MMA, NYPL, Chapel Hill, Philadelphia
   BM, Paris, Berlin-Dahlem, Vienna, Rotterdam, Hamburg, Prague

14.
Christ and the Woman of Samaria
 Dimensions:
  14¼ x 20⅜ inches.
 Blocks, 3:
  Buff, greenish yellow, black.
  After a Bolognese master. Weigel described this as a "beautiful" chiaroscuro by Jackson.

                      MFA

15.
Romulus and Remus, Wolf and Sea God
 Dimensions:
  2¾ x 7½ inches.
 Blocks, 2:
  Green, black.
  Attributed to Jackson. Probably an illustration for a book.

                       BM

16.
The Death of St Peter Martyr, after Titian   [Le Bl. 16, N. 10]
 Dimensions:
  21¼ x 13½ inches.
 Blocks, 4:
  Buff, pale greenish gray, brown, dark gray.
 Inscription, lower left (inside border):
  "*J: B: Jackson Sculp: & Excudit Venetiis* 1739."
 Outside bottom frame, center:
  "TITIANUS VECELLIUS CAD. INVENIT & PINXIT."
 The painting was destroyed by fire in 1867.

17.
The Presentation in the Temple (The Circumcision), after Veronese

[Le Bl. 4, N. 15]

 Dimensions:
  21⅛ x 15⅛ inches.
 Blocks, 4:
  Buff, reddish gray, dark gray, dark brown.
 Inscription, bottom:
  "*Illustrissimo, & Erudito Viro* CAROLO FREDERICK *Armigero, liberalium Artium Patrono,/*PAULI CAGLIARI *praeclarum hoc Opus in Ligno coelatum, in grati animi argumentum humiliter* D. D. D./*J: B: Jackson.*"
 1739.

18.
The Massacre of the Innocents, after Tintoretto   [Le Bl. 5]

 Dimensions:
  15½ x 21 inches.
 Blocks, 4:
  Buff, violet-gray, light brown, dark violet-brown.
 Inscription, center bottom:
  "*Illustrissimo, / et Praeclaro Viro Dno. Dno. /* SMART LETHIEULLIER / *Erudita Antiquitatis Studioso / Investigatori, Tabellam hanc /* JACOBI ROBUSTI *in sui / obsequium* D. D. D. *J: B: Jackson.*"
 1739.

19.
The Entombment, after Jacopo Bassano   [Le Bl. 12, N. 5]

 Dimensions:
  21⅞ x 15¼ inches.
 Blocks, 4:
  Buff, light reddish tan, gray, dark brown.
 Inscription on urn, above lower right-hand corner:
  "*J: B: Jackson Delin Sculp & excudit 1739*"
 Across bottom:
  "*Insignem hanc Tabulam a* JACOBO DE PONTE *depictam. Clarissimo Viro* JACOBO FACCIOLATO *Seminarii Patavini Præsidi; Archigymnasii ornamenta/ingenii doctrinæ, & in primis Latinæ eloquentia laude celeberrimo J B Jackson D. C.*"

20.

Holy Family and Four Saints, after Veronese

Dimensions:
22⅛ x 13⅝ inches.
Blocks, 4:
Light yellow, light greenish gray, dark brown, dark gray.
Inscription, bottom center:
"*Perillustri et Nobili Viro D^{no}D^{no}*/Bourchier Wrey Barronetto/*Generoso Artium Liberalium Fautori*/*in sui Obsequium* D. D. D. *J. B. Jackson*/*P: C: Veroneſe Pinxit.*".
1739.

21.

The Mystic Marriage of St Catherine, after Veronese [Le Bl. 18, N. 4]

Dimensions:
22 x 15¼ inches.
Blocks, 4:
Pale greenish gray, pale violet-gray, medium greenish gray, deep cold gray.
Inscription, lower center:
"Gulielmo Windham/*Armigero, Artium Elegantiorum*/*Fautori, hanc Tabulam humillime*/*Dedicat*/*J. B. Jackson.*"
Bottom left:
"*Paulo Veroneſe Pinxit J B J f 1740*"
Many impressions are found in brown tones.

22.

The Crucifixion, after Tintoretto [Le Bl. 9, N. 13]

Dimensions:
21½ x 16¼ inches (left plate), 22¾ x 16⅜ inches (center plate), 21½ x 16½ inches (right plate).
Blocks, 4:
Buff, light brown, gray, reddish brown.
Inscription, bottom center (center plate):
"*Illustrissimo & Nob: Viro D^{no}: D^{no}:*/Richardo Boyle *Comti de Burlington & Cork &c.*/*Magnæ Britanniæ & Hiberniæ Pari, Hiberniæ Archi-thesaurario*/*Heredetario, Nobilisimi Ordinis Periscelidis Equiti &c.*/*Optimæ Architecturæ Instauratori ac Cæterarum Artium Liberalium*/*Moecenati munificentissimo.*/*Singo-*

lare hoc Opus a JACOBO ROBUSTI depictam in Schola S: ROCCI Venetiis/adservatum. J: B: Jackson Anglus qui Ligno Coelavit humillime D. D. C. 1741."

On shield, bottom center (center plate):

"HONI SOIT·QUI·MAL Y PENSE·"

Below shield, bottom center (center plate):

"HONOR· VIRTUTIS· PREMIUM."

A bust portrait of a man in 18th-century dress is visible on the right knee of the woman with a child in the center background of the left sheet. It is not a likeness of Richard Boyle. Could this be a self-portrait by Jackson?

A trial proof of the key block, center sheet, is in the Rosenwald Collection, National Gallery of Art.

23.
Miracle of St. Mark, after Tintoretto [Le Bl. 15, N. 2]
Dimensions:
22¼ x 17¾ inches (left sheet), 22¼ x 17¾ inches (right sheet).
Blocks, 4:
Buff, light brown, dark brown, dark gray.
Inscription, lower left (left sheet):
"*Per illustri D^{no} D^{no}/EDUARDO WRIGHT,/Armigero,/pulcrarum Artium ex-/cultori vel sollertissimo,/hoc Jacobi Robusti/(communiter Tintoretto)/præclarum opus in/suæ argumentum ob-/servantiæ addicit, et/consecrat J. B. Jackfon.*"

24.
The Marriage at Cana, after Veronese
Dimensions:
23 x 16¾ inches (left sheet), 23 x 16¾ inches (right sheet).
Blocks, 4:
Buff, dark buff, violet-brown, dark brown.
Inscription, lower left (left sheet):
"*Paulo Cagliari/Veron: Pinxit.*"
Lower right (right sheet):
"Rev^{mo}· D^{no}· P./LEOPOLDO CAPELLO Coenobii D: GEORGII/Ord: S: Benedict:/ABBATI/ *meritissimo./J: B: Jackson*/D. D. D."
Extreme lower right (right sheet):
"*J: B: Jackson Delin: Sculp./& excudit Venetiis 1740.*"

Jackson in the *Enquiry* (p. 48) described this print, and the two preceding subjects, as being "in *Hugo's* Manner with Improvements."

25.

Presentation of the Virgin in the Temple, after Titian [Le Bl. 3, N. 18]

Dimensions:

22 x 15¾ inches (left sheet), 22 x 17⅞ inches (center sheet), 22 x 17¼ inches (right sheet).

Blocks, 4:

Light grayish umber, medium brown, dark gray, dark brown.

Inscription, lower left (left sheet):

"*Opus hoc admiratione sane dignum, cunctorumq; approbatione/commendatum, ac Sacrarii Confratrum Caritatis Venetiarum/potiſſimum ornamentum, a* Titiano Viccellio *Cadorensi,/Viro pingendi arte præ cæteris celeberrimo, coloribus quam/fieri potest ad naturale expressum, adumbratumq; pro viribus/exscribere studens J: B: Jackſon delineavit, excudit, et exſculpsit.* 1742."

Lower right, on streamer (right sheet):

"Ducit· Amor Patriæ."

Lower right, in block (right sheet):

"*Per Illuſtri, ac Nobili Viro D:ⁿᵒ D:ⁿᵒ/*Erasmo Philipps Barronetto/ *Artium zelantissimo Fautori, et de re litteraria/optime merito, Tabulam hanc tenue debitæ venerationis/suæ argumentum, emeritissimo Patrono, et Mecænati/ commendat, et dicat/J: B: Jackſon.*"

26.

The Virgin in the Clouds and Six Saints, after Titian [Le Bl. 14, N. 17]

Dimensions:

23¼ x 14¾ inches.

Blocks, 2:

Buff, black.

Inscription, upper left and right:

"*Ill*ᵐᵒ *atq; Excell:*ᵐᵒ *D:*ⁿᵒ *D:*ⁿᵒ Philippo Farsetti *Nob. Ven./Tabellam hanc a* Titiano Viccellio *jam depictam in/gratissimi animi, cultusq; perpetui testimonium,/Mecænati, ac Sospiti munificentissimo/humiliat, et consecrat J. B.* Jackſon."

Center of picture, on wall:

"Titianus Faciebat"

Bottom center:

"*J. B. Jackson Del: sculp:&c.* 1742."

Niccolò Boldrini's woodcut after Titian's drawing of the lower half of this subject (Le Bl. 12) evidently inspired Jackson to transcribe the entire painting as a pen-and-ink drawing in Titian's style, with a tint block added.

27.
The Descent of the Holy Spirit, after Titian [Le Bl. 13, N. 1]
   Dimensions:
      22 3/8 x 15 1/8 inches.
   Blocks, 4:
      Buff, light gray-brown, light yellow-brown, dark brown.
   Inscription, upper left and right:
      "*Perilluſtri, ac Nobili Viro* D.^{no} D.^{no} Jacobo Stewart Mackinzie,/*Honorabili Magnæ Britan-niæ Conſilii Conſcripto Patri*/*Opus hoc, quod ex* Titi-ani Viccellii *Pictura,/exſcripsit, in humillimi obſequii testi-/monium devo-vebat*/J. B. Jackſon."

28.
The Finding of Moses, after Veronese [Le Bl. 2, N.14]
   Dimensions:
      22 x 15 inches.
   Blocks, 4:
      Buff, light brown, light violet-gray, dark gray.
   Inscription, lower right:
      "*Illmo et Excell^{mo}* D: D:/Everardo Fawkener *Eq Aur/pro Mag: Brit: Rege ad Turc: Imper:/Legato. Elegant: Artium Moecena-/ti Munificentis: in sui Obsequii. Ar-/gumentum humill:* D: D:/J: B: Jackson."
   Lower left:
      "*Ex Tabella/a* Paulo Calliari *Veron^s./depicta penes* J: Smith *Ven*/J: B: *Jackson Del Sculp & excud/1741.*"

29.
The Raising of Lazarus, after Leandro Bassano [Le Bl. 6, N. 7]
   Dimensions:
      23 1/2 x 14 7/8 inches.
   Blocks, 4:
      Buff, light reddish gray, gray, dark cold brown.
   Inscription, upper left and right:
      "*Ill:^{mo}* D:^{no} D:^{no} Vincentio Riccardi, *Marchioni/Florentino, amplissimo Senatori,/amænarum litterarum scientiarumq; excultori/peramantissimo, Tabellam hanc a/*Leandro *de* Ponte *colori-/bus expressam veluti exigu-/um obser-vantiæ suæ/specimen* D. D. D./J B Jackson"
   Center bottom:
      "*J: B: Jackſon Del. ſculp. &c. 1742.*"

30.

Christ on the Mount of Olives, after Jacopo Bassano [Le Bl. 8, N. 6]

Dimensions:

22 x 15⅛ inches.

Blocks, 4:

Buff, medium brown, gray, dark brown.

Inscription, bottom:

"Ill:ᵐᵃᵉ atq; Excell:ᵐᵃᵉ D:ⁿᵃᵉ D:ⁿᵃᵉ/*Paulinæ Contarenæ*/Nᴏʙ: Vᴇɴᴇᴛᴀᴇ, *aviti sanguinis ingenti splendore claræ, sed Virtutum nobilitate longe clariori, piissimum/ hoc Christianæ Fidei monumentum, exiguum obsequentissimæ servitutis suæ signum, quod ex pictura*/Jacobi de Ponte *delineavit, et exfculpsit, generossimæ Patronæ, et Auspici dedicabat J: B: Jackson.*".

1743.

A trial proof of the key block is in the Rosenwald Collection, National Gallery of Art.

31.

Melchisedech Blessing Abraham, after Francesco Bassano [Le Bl. 1, N. 19]

Dimensions:

22½ x 15⅛ inches.

Blocks, 4:

Buff, warm gray, brown, dark brown.

Inscription, lower right:

"*Per-illustri* D.ⁿᵒ D.ⁿᵒ/Jᴏᴀɴɴɪ Rᴇᴀᴅᴇ/*Tabellam hanc in obfe-/quentiffimæ reverentiæ/specimen D. D. D./J. B. Jackfon/ex Tabella penes/D. Jos*ʰ *Smith.*"

1743.

32.

Dives and Lazarus (The Rich Man and Lazarus), after Jacopo Bassano

Dimensions:

22 x 15 inches (left sheet), 22 x 15 inches (right sheet).

Blocks, 4:

Buff, light brown, light brownish gray, dark brownish gray

Inscription, lower left of left plate:

"*Per-illustri, ac Honorabili Viro*/D:ⁿᵒ D:ⁿᵒ Rᴏʙᴇʀᴛᴏ Hᴏʙʟʏɴ,/*Armigero, Magnæq; Britan-/niæ Consilii Conscripto Patri,/Artium, Scientiarumq; Cultori,/et Mæcenati, sui ergo obsequii/dicabat*/J. B. Jackfon."

Lower right of left plate:

"*Ab Exemplari, Jacobi de Ponte, quod Venetiis penes/D. Joseph Smith extat, exscripsit qui dicabat./J: Basan P:ͬ*"

1743.

33.

Algernon Sidney, after Justus Verus [Le Bl. 20]

Dimensions:

13⅜ x 8¾ inches with letters, 8½ x 7½ inches (oval portrait only).

Blocks, 4:

Tan, light brown, light gray, dark gray.

Inscription, left and right under oval:

"*Zustus Verus, pinx: J: B: J: sculp; et exc:*"

In rectangle at bottom:

" At the Time when Mr. ALGERNON SIDNEY *was* Ambassador
" at that Court, Monsieur TERLON *the* French *Ambassador,*
" had the Confidence to tear out of the Book of Mottos
" in the King's Library, this Verse, which Mr. Sidney
" (according to the Liberty allowed to all Noble Strangers)
" had written in it:/
" Manus haec inimica Tyrannis
" Ense petit placidam sub Libertate quietem.
" Though Monsieur Terlon *understood not a word of*
" Latin, he was told by others the meaning of that Sen-
" tence, which he considered as a Libel *upon the* French
" Government and upon such as was then setting up in
" Denmark *by* French *Assistance* or Example.

Pref: to *Acco:ͭ of Denmark* 4.:ᵗʰ *Edit:P:23.*

Another version with light red in place of light gray (Philadelphia, which also has set of progressive proofs).

Smithsonian Institution (U.S. National Museum)
Worcester, MFA, Fogg, Baltimore, MMA, NYPL, Philadelphia
BM, Berlin-Dahlem, Brussels, Frankfurt, Hamburg

34.
Antique Bust of Woman
>Dimensions:
>>14⅞ x 10½ inches (irregular oval).
>
>Blocks, 4:
>>Yellow-gray, greenish brown, gray-brown, brown.

MFA

35.
Lovers (facing right), perhaps after Piazzetta
>Dimensions:
>>15 x 10½ inches.
>
>Blocks, 5:
>>Light brownish gray, darker brownish gray, medium brown, cold gray, dark brown.
>>Attributed to Jackson.

V&A

36.
Lovers (woman full face), perhaps after Piazzetta
>Dimensions:
>>15 x 10½ inches.
>
>Blocks, 5:
>>Light brownish gray, darker brownish gray, medium brown, cold gray, dark brown.
>>Companion piece to previous print. Attributed to Jackson.

V&A

37.
Lamentation Over the Body of Christ
>Dimensions:
>>20½ x 13¼ inches.
>
>Blocks, 5 or 6:
>>Blue, brown, red, flesh, gray.
>
>Inscription, bottom:
>>"*Et tuam ipſius animam pertranſibit gladius,*"
>>This is probably an experiment in color printing made by Jackson, after his own design, before attempting the Ricci set.

BM

38.
Heroic Landscape With Dedication and Classical Ruins, after Marco Ricci
[Le Bl. 21–25, N.20–25a]

Dimensions:
16¾ x 23⅛ inches.
Blocks, 7 to 10:
Tones of blue, buff, gray-violet, green and dark gray.
Inscription in tablet at lower left:
"Ill*mo*, atq; Excell*mo* D*no* D*no*/Roberto D'Arcy,/Comiti de Holderneſſe *&c. &c. &c.*/Apud Sereniſs Remp: Venetam pro Mag:/Britan· Rege Legato Extraordinario./Hoc noviſſime excogitatum Opus in humillimi/obsequii teſtimonium dedicabat/J. B. Jackſon.".
1744.
A copy in the Museum of Fine Arts, Boston, has D'Arcy's coat-of-arms on the entablature of the arch to the right with red and blue notes. The British Museum has a copy with brownish-red touched in with water colors in the clothing of the men under the arch.
Reichel reproduced this in full size and color (plate 98).

MFA, MMA, BM, Venice

39.
Heroic Landscape With Sheep, Statues, and Gentlemen, after Marco Ricci
[Le Bl. 21–25, N. 20–25b]

Dimensions:
16¾ x 23⅛ inches.
Blocks, 7 to 10:
1744.
Colors vary in different impressions.

Smithsonian Institution (U.S. National Museum)
MFA, BM, Venice

40.
Heroic Landscape with Fisherman, Cows, and Horsemen, after Marco Ricci
[Le Bl. 21–25, N. 20–25c]

Dimensions:
16½ x 23 inches.
Blocks, 7 to 10:
Colors vary in different impressions.
1744.

MFA, MMA, Worcester, BM, V&A, Berlin-Dahlem, Venice, Brussels

41.

Heroic Landscape with Cart and Goatherd, with S. Giorgio Maggiore in Background, after Marco Ricci [Le Bl. 21–25, N. 20–25d]
    Dimensions:
        16½ x 23 inches.
    Blocks, 7 to 10:
        Colors vary in different impressions.
    1744.

                                              MFA, BM, Venice, Dresden

42.

Heroic Landscape with Women at Brook, Child Fishing, and Herdsmen, after Marco Ricci [Le Bl. 21–25, N. 20–25e]
    Dimensions:
        16¾ x 23½ inches.
    Blocks, 7 to 10:
        Colors vary in different impressions.
    1744.
        Reichel reproduced this in full size and color (plate 99).

                                MMA, MFA, BM, Venice, Milan, Berlin-Dahlem

43.

Heroic Landscape with Watering Place, Riders, and Obelisk, after Marco Ricci
    Dimensions:
        16⅝ x 23¼ inches.
    Blocks, 7 to 10:
        Colors vary in different impressions.
    1744.

                                                MFA, MMA, BM, V&A, Venice

44.

Battle near Parma, after Francesco Simonini
    Dimensions:
        20 x 40 inches (two joined sheets)
    Blocks, 7 or 8:
        Buff, brown, light green, blue-green, light transparent red, deep red, dark gray.
    1752.

The only known copy is in the British Museum. Tone has darkened and paper is torn in parts. This print is described in the *Enquiry*. Jackson erroneously referred to this artist as "Simonnetta."

BM

45.

Ornamental Border with Fruit, Flowers, and Purple Grapes
   Dimensions:
      $6\frac{1}{4}$ x $25\frac{7}{8}$ inches.
   Blocks, 4:
      Red, blue, yellow, green.
      Print for wallpaper.

BM

46.

Ornamental Border with Fruit, Flowers, and Green Grapes
   Dimensions:
      $6\frac{3}{8}$ x $25\frac{7}{8}$ inches.
   Blocks, 4:
      Red, blue, yellow and green.
      Print for wallpaper.

BM

47.

Ornamental Frame with Flowers and Fruit
   Dimensions:
      $24\frac{3}{4}$ x $18\frac{1}{2}$ inches.
   Blocks, 4:
      Red, blue, yellow, gray-green.
      Print for wallpaper.

BM

48.

Ornamental Frame with Fruit
   Dimensions:
      $25\frac{1}{8}$ x $17\frac{1}{4}$ inches.
   Blocks, 4:
      Red, blue, yellow, gray-green.
      Print for wallpaper.

BM

49.

Ornamental Frame with Flowers and Girl's Head

    Dimensions:
        26 x 18½ inches.
    Blocks, 4:
        Red, blue, yellow, green.
        Print for wallpaper. Central figure is described under No. 59.

                                                                                                  BM

50.

Dancing Nymph with Bow and Arrows

    Dimensions:
        11⅛ x 6⅜ inches.
    Blocks, 2:
        Olive green, black.
        Print for wallpaper. Probably cut by Jackson as a guide for his workshop. See Nos. 59–74.

                Smithsonian Institution (U.S. National Museum)

51.

Bust of Democritus

    Dimensions:
        9¼ x 7½ inches (sheet size).
    Blocks, 4:
        Buff, light gray, medium gray, dark gray.
        Plate from Jackson, *An Essay on the Invention of Engraving and Printing in Chiaro Oscuro*, 1754.

52.

The Lion

    Dimensions:
        9¼ x 7½ inches.
    Blocks, 6:
        Yellow, red, light green, blue-gray, light gray, dark gray-green.
        Plate from Jackson, *Essay* . . . , 1754. This subject was copied from plate 34 of Giorgio Fossati, *Raccolta di varie favole*, Venice, 1744.

53.
Building and Vegetable
>Dimensions:
>>9¼ x 7½ inches.
>
>Blocks, 6:
>>Yellow, light green, light red, crimson, light gray, dark gray.
>>Plate from Jackson, *Essay* . . . , 1754.

54.
Statue of Apollo
>Dimensions:
>>9¼ x 7½ inches.
>
>Blocks, 4:
>>Light buff, medium buff, gray, and dark gray.
>>Plate from Jackson, *Essay* . . . , 1754.

55.
The Farnese Hercules
>Dimensions:
>>9¼ x 7½ inches.
>
>Blocks, 4:
>>Buff, greenish buff, gray, dark greenish gray.
>>Plate from Jackson, *Essay* . . . , 1754.

56.
Antique Bust of a Man
>Dimensions:
>>9¼ x 7½ inches.
>
>Blocks, 4:
>>Buff, gray-brown, gray, dark greenish gray.
>>Plate from Jackson, *Essay* . . . , 1754.

57.
Pheasant and Garden Urn

Dimensions:
9¼ x 7½ inches.

Blocks, 7:
Yellow, light green, warm gray, blue-gray, light red, crimson, dark gray-green.

Plate from Jackson, *Essay* . . . , 1754.

58.
Ruin of Garden Temple

Dimensions:
9¼ x 7½ inches.

Blocks, 7:
Yellow, light green, warm gray, cold gray, light red, crimson, dark gray-green.

Plate from Jackson, *Essay* . . . , 1754.

Jackson's Workshop

59.
Woman Standing Holding Apron, after S. Le Clerc

Dimensions:
11¼ x 6½ inches (sheet size).

Blocks, 2:
Deep red and pale green.

Print for wallpaper. This figure appears in the center of the ornamental frame, No. 49 in this catalog, in the British Museum impression. After a plate in the series of etchings by Sébastien Le Clerc, *Les Figures à la mode*, 1685. The figure is reversed.

BM

60

Female Statue with Fruit and Wheat
>Dimensions:
>11¼ x 6½ inches.
>Blocks, 2:
>>Deep red and yellow.
>>Print for wallpaper.

                     Philadelphia

61.

Female Statue with Mask
>Dimensions:
>11¼ x 6½ inches.
>Blocks, 2:
>>Deep red and yellow.
>>Print for wallpaper.

                     Philadelphia

62.

Queen with Armor and Model of Building
>Dimensions:
>11¼ x 6½ inches.
>Blocks, 2:
>>Deep red and pale green.
>>Print for wallpaper. In the style of Villamena.

                     Philadelphia

63.

Apollo with Lyre
>Dimensions:
>11¼ x 6½ inches.
>Blocks, 2:
>Green and black. Also deep red and yellow.
>Print for wallpaper.

         Smithsonian Institution (U.S. National Museum)
                     Philadelphia

64.

Woman with Shepherd's Pipe

    Dimensions:
        11¼ x 6½ inches.
    Blocks, 2:
        Deep red and yellow.
        Print for wallpaper.

                                              Philadelphia

65.

Woman with Sheet of Music and Horn

    Dimensions:
        11¼ x 6½ inches.
    Blocks, 2:
        Deep red and pale green. Also red and yellow.
        Print for wallpaper.

                                              Philadelphia

66.

Woman with Pitcher and Apron, after S. Le Clerc

    Dimensions:
        11¼ x 6½ inches.
    Blocks, 2:
        Deep red and pale green.
        Print for wallpaper. After a plate in the series of 24 etchings by Sébastien Le Clerc, *Les Figures à la mode*, 1685. The figure is reversed.

                                              Philadelphia

67.

Old Woman Standing, after S. Le Clerc

    Dimensions:
        11¼ x 6½ inches.
    Blocks, 2:
        Deep red and pale green.
        Print for wallpaper. After a plate in the series of 24 etchings by Sébastien Le Clerc, *Les Figures à la mode*, 1685. The figure is reversed.

                                              Philadelphia

68.

Lady with Staff
    Dimensions:
        11¼ x 6½ inches.
    Blocks, 2:
        Deep red and yellow.
        Print for wallpaper.

                                            Philadelphia

69.

Woman with Fruit and Basket
    Dimensions:
        11¼ x 6½ inches.
    Blocks, 2:
        Deep red and pale green. Also red and yellow.
        Print for wallpaper. In the style of Villamena.

                                            BM

70.

Woman with Branches and Incense Burner
    Dimensions:
        11¼ x 6½ inches.
    Blocks, 2:
        Deep red and pale green. Also red and yellow.
        Print for wallpaper. In the style of Villamena.

                                            BM

71.

Woman with Flowers and Vines
    Dimensions:
        11¼ x 6½ inches.
    Blocks, 2:
        Red and green. Also red and yellow.
        Print for wallpaper. In the style of Villamena.

                                            BM

72.

Standing Woman, Head Turned to Right, after Watteau

    Dimensions:
      11 x 5 inches.
    Blocks, 2:
      Green and black.
      Print for wallpaper. After Boucher's etching after a drawing by Watteau (plate 216 in Jean de Julienne's compilation of Watteau's work, *Figures de différents caractères*, ca. 1740).

                                                                MMA, Philadelphia, BM

73.

Lady with Fan, after S. Le Clerc

    Dimensions:
      11 x 4½ inches.
    Blocks, 2:
      Green and black.
      Print for wallpaper. After a plate in the series of 24 etchings by Sébastien Le Clerc, *Les Figures à la mode*, 1685. The figure is reversed and the fan has been shifted to the upper hand.

                                                                        MMA

74.

Classical Female Statue

    Dimensions:
      11¼ x 6½ inches.
    Blocks, 2:
      Deep red and yellow.
      Print for wallpaper.

                                                                    Philadelphia, MMA

75.
Boy Looking Down

> Dimensions:
> 3 x 2 inches.
> Blocks, 2:
> Light brown and black.
> Perhaps after Piazzetta.

MFA, BM

76.
Lady with a Flower

> Dimensions:
> 14¾ x 11¼ inches.
> Blocks, 3:
> Buff, light brown, brown.
> Possibly after Kneller. Very weak and crude.

BM, V&A

Unverified Subjects

77.
The Annunciation, after Parmigianino

> Dimensions:
> 6¾ x 4⅝ inches.
> Blocks, 3:
> Tones of brown.
> This is listed as Jackson's in Gutekunst & Klipstein's catalogue 40, 1938. It is described as having "the initials and an engraved letter border," but whether the initials are Jackson's or Parmigianino's is uncertain.

78.

St. Peter and St. Paul Surprised by the Executioner, after Titian

[Le Bl. 17, N. 16]

Le Blanc and Nagler list this print in addition to *St. Peter Martyr*, but most likely it is the same subject. The title might have been taken from a museum catalogue which listed the identical print under a different title.

79.

The Entombment, after Titian [Le Bl. 11]

This is included in Le Blanc (*J. C. mis au tombeau*) but it seems likely that it was confused with Bassano's identically titled subject.

80.

Giovanni Gastro I De Medici

This is listed as a Jackson print in Berlin-Dahlem but has not been located.

81.

Elisabeth, Duchess of Hamilton, as a Shepherdess

This is catalogued as a Jackson print in the Dresden Kunstsammlungen but was lost in the war.

The *Chiaroscuros*
and *Color Woodcuts* of
John Baptist Jackson

THO. HOLLIS *Arm. Hospit.* Lincoln. D. D. D. *J. B. Jackson sculptor.*

1. CHRIST GIVING THE KEYS TO ST. PETER, after Raphael (See also color plate)

2. VENUS AND CUPID WITH A BOW, after Parmigianino (See also color plate)

100

3. WOMAN STANDING HOLDING JAR ON HER HEAD, after Parmigianino

5. WOMAN MEDITATING (ST. THAIS?), after etching by Parmigianino (See also color plate)

7. BOOKPLATE

6. Ulysses and Polyphemus, after Primaticcio

8. Judgment of Solomon, after Rubens

9. THE VISITATION, after Annibale Carracci

10. JULIUS CAESAR, after Titian

11. St. Rocco, after Cherubino Alberti

12. STATUETTE OF NEPTUNE, after Giovanni da Bologna

14. Christ and the Woman of Samaria

15. ROMULUS AND REMUS, WOLF, AND SEA GOD

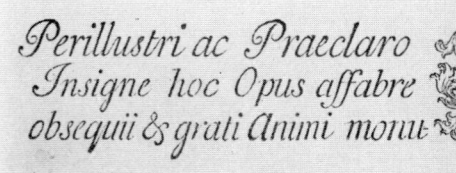

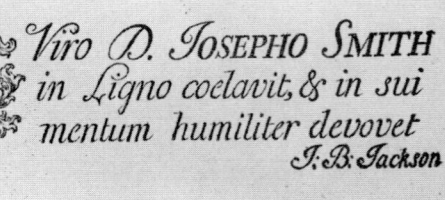

13. DESCENT FROM THE CROSS, after Rembrandt (See also color plate)

16. THE DEATH OF ST. PETER MARTYR, after Titian

17. The Presentation in the Temple (The Circumcision), after Veronese

18. The Massacre of the Innocents, after Tintoretto

22. THE CRUCIFIXION, after Tintoretto, center sheet (See also color plates)

22. THE CRUCIFIXION, after Tintoretto, left sheet   (See also color plates)

22. THE CRUCIFIXION, after Tintoretto, right sheet   (See also color plates)

19. THE ENTOMBMENT, after Jacopo Bassano

20. HOLY FAMILY AND FOUR SAINTS, after Veronese

21. THE MYSTIC MARRIAGE OF ST. CATHERINE, after Veronese

26. THE VIRGIN IN THE CLOUDS AND SIX SAINTS, after Titian

23. MIRACLE OF ST. MARK, after Tintoretto, left sheet

122

23. MIRACLE OF ST. MARK, after Tintoretto, right sheet

123

24. THE MARRIAGE AT CANA, after Veronese, left sheet

24. THE MARRIAGE AT CANA, after Veronese, right sheet

27. THE DESCENT OF THE HOLY SPIRIT, after Titian

28. THE FINDING OF MOSES, after Veronese

29. THE RAISING OF LAZARUS, after Leandro Bassano

31. MELCHISEDECH BLESSING ABRAHAM, after Francesco Bassano

32. DIVES AND LAZARUS (THE RICH MAN AND LAZARUS), after Jacopo Bassano, left sheet

32. DIVES AND LAZARUS (THE RICH MAN AND LAZARUS), after Jacopo Bassano, right sheet

131

30. CHRIST ON THE MOUNT OF OLIVES, after Jacopo Bassano

37. LAMENTATION OVER THE BODY OF CHRIST

33. ALGERNON SIDNEY, after Justus Verus

34. ANTIQUE BUST OF WOMAN

25. Presentation of the Virgin in the Temple, after Titian, center sheet

25. PRESENTATION OF THE VIRGIN IN THE TEMPLE, after Titian, left sheet

25. Presentation of the Virgin in the Temple, after Titian, right sheet

137

35. LOVERS (facing right), perhaps after Piazzetta

36. LOVERS (woman full face), perhaps after Piazzetta

38. Heroic Landscape With Dedication and Classical Ruins, after Marco Ricci

39. Heroic Landscape With Sheep, Statues, and Gentlemen, after Marco Ricci

40. HEROIC LANDSCAPE WITH FISHERMAN, COWS, AND HORSEMEN, after Marco Ricci (See also color plates)

41. HEROIC LANDSCAPE WITH CART AND GOATHERD, AND WITH S. GIORGIO MAGGIORE IN BACKGROUND, after Marco Ricci

42. Heroic Landscape With Women at Brook, Child Fishing, and Herdsmen, after Marco Ricci

43. Heroic Landscape with Watering Place, Riders, and Obelisk, after Marco Ricci (See also color plate)

44. BATTLE NEAR PARMA, after Francesco Simonini

44. Battle Near Parma, after Francesco Simonini, detail

45. Ornamental Border With Fruit, Flowers, and Purple Grapes

46. Ornamental Border With Fruit, Flowers, and Green Grapes

47. ORNAMENTAL FRAME WITH FLOWERS AND FRUIT

48. Ornamental Frame With Fruit

49. ORNAMENTAL FRAME WITH FLOWERS AND GIRL'S HEAD   (See also color plate)
59. WOMAN STANDING HOLDING APRON, after S. Le Clerc

50. Dancing Nymph With Bow and Arrows

51. BUST OF DEMOCRITUS

52. THE LION

53. BUILDING AND VEGETABLE   (See also color plate)

54. STATUE OF APOLLO

55. THE FARNESE HERCULES

56. ANTIQUE BUST OF A MAN

57. PHEASANT AND GARDEN URN

58. Ruin of Garden Temple

60. Female Statue With Fruit and Wheat

61. Female Statue With Mask

161

62. Queen With Armor and Model of Building

63. Apollo With Lyre

64. WOMAN WITH SHEPHERD'S PIPE   65. WOMAN WITH SHEET OF MUSIC AND HORN

66. Woman With Pitcher and Apron, after S. Le Clerc

67. Old Woman Standing, after S. Le Clerc

68. LADY WITH STAFF   69. WOMAN WITH FRUIT AND BASKET

165

70. WOMAN WITH BRANCHES AND INCENSE BURNER

71. WOMAN WITH FLOWERS AND VINES

72. STANDING WOMAN, HEAD TURNED TO RIGHT, after Watteau

73. LADY WITH FAN, after S. Le Clerc

74. CLASSICAL FEMALE STATUE

76. LADY WITH A FLOWER

75. BOY LOOKING DOWN

BIBLIOGRAPHY

Anonymous. *An Enquiry into the Origins of Printing in Europe, by a Lover of Art.* London, 1752.
   A rewrite of Jackson's manuscript journal, with some sections quoted verbatim. The artist's career from about 1725 to 1752 is described. The most important biographical source and a rare book.

Audin, M. *Essai sur les graveurs de bois en France au dix-huitième siècle.* Paris, 1925, pp. 99–102.
   Contains a section listing many books illustrated by Jackson in Paris, mostly in later editions.

Baverel, P. *Notices sur les graveurs*, Besançon, 1807, vol. 1, pp. 341–342.

Bénézit, E. *Dictionnaire des peintres, sculpteurs, dessinateurs, & graveurs.* Paris, 1924 (1st ed. 1913), vol. 2, p. 693.

Bewick, Thomas. *Memoir of Thomas Bewick, Written by Himself,* 1822–1828. New York, 1925 (1st ed., 1862), pp. 213–214.
   Mentions meeting Jackson in advanced age, about 1777. The book contains much personal reminiscence and observation on life but little concrete detail for the student.

Bigmore, E. C. and Wyman, C. W. H. *A Bibliography of Printing.* London, 1880–1886, vol. 1, pp. 201, 365.
   The most extensive annotated listing of books relating to printing. Has a description of Jackson's *Essay*.

Brulliot, F. *Dictionnaire des monogrammes.* Munich, 1832–1834, vol. 2, Nos. 1288, 1352, 1535.

Bryan, M. *Dictionary of Painters and Engravers.* London and New York, 1904 (1st ed. 1816), vol. 3, p. 99.
   The most comprehensive biographical dictionary of artists in the English language.

Burch, R. M. *Colour Printing and Colour Printers.* London, 1910, pp. 72–77.
   The most comprehensive general survey, but with more than occasional inaccuracies. There is a lack of sensitivity in art matters. These comments apply also to the section on Jackson.

Chatto, W., and Jackson, J. *A Treatise on Wood-Engraving.* London, 1861 (1st. ed. 1839), pp. 453–457.
   The classic work on the subject; scholarly, objective, and voluminously illustrated. Has the fullest early account of Jackson and is the basis for most later studies of the artist.

Cust, L. "John Baptist Jackson," *Dictionary of National Biography.* New York and London, 1885–1900, vol. 29, p. 100.

De Boni, F. *Biografia degli artisti.* Venice, 1840, p. 499.

Donnell, Edna. "The Van Rensselaer Wall Paper and J. B. Jackson—A Study in Disassociation." *Metropolitan Museum Studies,* 1932, vol. 4, pp. 77–108.
   The most scholarly study of Jackson's wallpaper career. Shows, by an examination of styles, that Jackson could not have made the wallpapers indiscriminately attributed to him.

Duplessis, G. *Histoire de la gravure.* Paris, 1880, pp. 314–315.

Entwisle, E. A. *The Book of Wallpaper.* London, 1954, pp. 65–67, 76.
   Contains new information on wallpaper manufacturers in London during the 18th century, some of it bearing on Jackson.

Frankau, J. *Eighteenth-Century Colour-Prints.* London, 1907, pp. 42–46.
   Has an appreciative section on Jackson, highly romanticized.

Friedländer, M. J. *Der Holzschnitt: Handbücher der Staatlichen Museen zu Berlin.* Berlin and Leipzig, 1926 (1st ed. 1917), pp. 224–226.

Fuessli, J. C. *Raisonirendes Verzeichniss der vornehmsten Kupferstecher.* Zurich, 1771, pp. 353–354.

Furst, H. *The Modern Woodcut.* New York, 1924, pp. 88, 99.
   A fine general survey, although judgments are occasionally dogmatic.

Gallo, R. *L'Incisioni nel '700 a Venezia e a Bassano.* Venice, 1941, pp. 22–23.
   A solid study containing some new material on the artists of the period.

Gori Gandellini, G. *Notizie Istoriche degl'Intagliatori.* Siena, 1771, vol. 2, p. 156.

Gusman, P. *La Gravure sur bois et d'epargne sur metal du XIVe au XXe siècle.* Paris, 1916, pp. 32, 164–165, 193, 252.

Hardie, Martin. *English Coloured Books.* New York and London, 1906, pp. 19–27.
   While a brief but sensitive account of Jackson is given, the main emphasis is on the *Essay* as an illustrated book.

Heinecken, C.H. von. *Idée générale d'une collection complette d'estampes.* Leipzig and Vienna, 1771, p. 94.

HELLER, J. *Geschichte der Holzschneidekunst.* Bamberg, 1823, pp. 295–296. *Praktisches Handbuch für Kupferstichsammler.* Leipzig, 1850, p. 334.
> Lists 10 chiaroscuros by Jackson.

HELLER, J., and ANDRESEN, A. *Handbuch für Kupferstichsammler.* Leipzig, 1870, vol. 1, pp. 706–707.
> Lists 11 prints by Jackson.

HUBER, M. *Notices générales des graveurs et des peintres.* Dresden, 1787, pp. 676, 698.

HUBER, M., and ROST, C. C. *Handbuch für Kunstliebhaber und Sammler.* Zurich, 1808, vol. 9, pp. 129–131.

HUBER, M., ROST, C. C., and MARTINI, C. G. *Manuel des curieux et des amateurs d'art.* Zurich, 1797–1808, vol. 9, pp. 121–123.
> First catalog of Jackson's work; lists 10 titles.

JACKSON, JOHN BAPTIST. *An Essay on the Invention of Engraving and Printing in Chiaro Oscuro, as Practised by Albert Durer, Hugo di Carpi, &c., and the Application of It to the Making Paper Hangings of Taste, Duration, and Elegance.* London, 1754.
> Written by Jackson to promote his wallpapers, it repeats some of his assertions in the *Enquiry* but gives little detail concerning his career. It is important as an illustrated book and as an early document in the history of wallpaper. The prints have suffered from the use of an inferior oil vehicle.

KAINEN, JACOB. "John Baptist Jackson and his Chiaroscuros." *Printing and Graphic Arts*, vol. 4, no. 4, 1956, pp. 85–92.
> An excerpt from the present work, then in progress, in a different version.

KREPLIN, B. C. "John Baptist Jackson," in Thieme, U., and Becker, F., *Allgemeines Lexikon der Bildenden Künstler.* Leipzig, 1907–1950, vol. 18, pp. 224–225.
> The most comprehensive biographical dictionary of artists. Has a good article on Jackson and a small bibliography.

LE BLANC, C. *Manuel de l'amateur d'estampes.* Paris, 1854–1888, vol. 2, p. 416.
> Particularly valuable for its catalogs of the work of engravers. With Nagler, contains the largest listing of Jackson's prints.

LEVIS, H. C. *A Descriptive Bibliography of Books in English Relating to Engraving and the Collection of Prints.* London, 1912, pp. 182–184.

LEWIS, C. T. C. *The Story of Picture Printing in England During the 19th Century; or Forty Years of Wood and Stone.* London, 1928, pp. 2, 21, 26, 34, 40, 43, 195.
> Written in an oppressively popular style with emphasis on Baxter and Le Blond. Jackson is mentioned often but sketchily as the distant ancestor of "picture printing."

LINTON, W. *The Masters of Wood Engraving*. London, 1889, p. 214.
   Discusses the subject from the standpoint of a late-19th-century technician. Nevertheless is open-minded, if slightly superior, about the chiaroscuro woodcut.

LONGHI, G. *Catalogo dei più celebri intagliatori in legno ed in rame*. Milan, 1821, p. 51.

MABERLY, J. *The Print Collector*. London, 1844, p. 130.
   The first American edition, New York, 1880, edited by Robert Hoe, copies the annotated description of the *Essay* from Bigmore and Wyman.

MCCLELLAND, N. *Historic Wall-Papers*. Philadelphia and London, 1924, pp. 47, 79, 141–154, 165, 324–329, 423.
   Makes many references to Jackson, largely inaccurate.

MIREUR, H. *Dictionnaire des ventes d'art fait en France*. Paris, 1911–1912, vol. 4, p. 23.

MÜLLER, F., and KLUNZINGER, K. *Die Künstler Aller Zeiten und Völker*. 1857–1864, vol. 2, p. 430.

MÜLLER, H. A., MÜLLER, H. W., and SINGER, H. W. *Allgemeines Künstler-Lexicon*. Frankfurt, 1895–1901, vol. 2, p. 240.

NAGLER, G. K. *Allgemeines Künstler-Lexicon*. Munich. 1835–52, vol. 6, pp. 383–384.
   The most extensive of all dictionaries of artists up to the time of Thieme and Becker, *q.v.* With Le Blanc, has the fullest catalog of Jackson's prints.
   Die Monogrammisten, Munich, 1858–1879, vol. 3, pp. 730, 836.

OMAN, C.C. *Catalogue of Wall-Papers*. London, Victoria and Albert Museum, 1929, pp. 24–25, 33.
   A good historical account which includes Jackson's contributions to the rise of scenic wallpaper.

PALLUCCHINI, RODOLFO, *Mostra degli incisori Veneti del settecento*. Venice, 1941, ed. 2, pp. 16, 103–104.
   Catalog of the exhibition held in Venice in 1941.

PAPILLON, J. M. *Traité historique et pratique de la gravure en bois*. Paris, 1766, vol. 1, pp. 323–324, 327–329, 415.
   Contains personal recollections of Jackson and his career in France. The book is valuable as the first technical treatise on the woodcut, but the historical section is notoriously inaccurate and heavily weighted with Papillon's prejudices.

PERCIVAL, MACIVER. "Jackson of Battersea and his Wall Papers." *The Connoisseur*, 1922, vol. 62, pp. 25–36.

REDGRAVE, S. *Dictionary of Artists of the English School.* London, 1874, p. 227.

REICHEL, ANTON. *Die Clair-Obscur-Schnitte des XVI., XVII. und XVIII. Jahrhunderts.* Zurich, Leipzig, and Vienna, 1926, p. 48.

    The finest work on chiaroscuro, with 100 magnificent facsimile illustrations in color, fully described, and black-and-white illustrations in the text. Reproduces two of Jackson's Ricci prints in actual size and color.

SAVAGE, W. *Practical Hints on Decorative Printing.* London, 1822, pp. 15–16.

    Savage was the first writer to acknowledge Jackson's contributions to color printing, although he was critical of his inks. The book attempts to show, through examples, that color printing from woodblocks is practical for a variety of purposes.

SMITH, J. *The Printers Grammar.* London, 1755, p. 136.

SPOONER, S. *Dictionary of Painters, Engravers, Sculptors & Architects.* New York, 1853, vol. 1, pp. 420–421.

STRUTT, J. *Dictionary of Engravers.* London, 1785–86, vol. 2, p. 41.

SUGDEN, A. V., and EDMONDSON, J.L. *A History of English Wallpaper.* New York and London, 1925, pp. 61–71.

    The most thorough book on the subject although the treatment of Jackson is narrowly confined, like most wallpaper books, to his shortcomings as a decorator for elegant homes.

WALPOLE, HORACE. *Anecdotes of Painting in England. A Catalogue of Engravers who Have Been Born, or Resided in England. Digested from the Manuscript of George Vertue.* London, 1765 (1st ed. 1762), p. 3.

    Important as the first compilation on this subject.

    The Letters of Horace Walpole. Edited by Mrs. Paget Toynbee, Oxford, 1903–05, vol. 3, p. 166.

WEIGEL, R. *Kunstlagercatalog.* Leipzig, 1837–1866, vol. 2, pp. 103, 105; vol. 4, p. 52.

WICK, PETER A. *Suite of Six Color Woodcuts of Heroic Landscapes by John Baptist Jackson after Marco Ricci.* 1955, 12 pp.

    Manuscript read at the XVIII Congres International d'Histoire de L'Art, Venice, Sept. 12–18, 1955. The first good, scholarly study of the Ricci prints. Traces Jackson's career briefly but accurately.

Y. D. Historical Remarks on Cutting in Wood. *The Gentleman's Magazine*, February 1752, vol. 22, pp. 78–79.

    The first published statement of Jackson's contribution as a woodcutter.

Zanetti, A. M. *Della pittura veneziana.* Venice, 1792 (1st ed. 1771), vol. 2, pp. 689, 716. Zanetti was the librarian of St. Mark's and the nephew of the famous chiaroscurist.

Zani, D. P. *Enciclopedia metodica delle belle arti.* Parma, 1817–24, vol. 11, p. 47.

Zanotto, F. *Nuovissimo guida di Venezia.* Venice, 1856, p. 320, note 3.

INDEX TO PLATES

1. *Christ Giving the Keys to St. Peter*, after Raphael, 55 (color), 99
2. *Venus and Cupid with a Bow*, after Parmigianino, 56 (color) 100
3. *Woman Standing Holding Jar on Her Head*, after Parmigianino, 101
5. *Woman Meditating (St. Thais?)*, after Parmigianino, 57 (color), 102
6. *Ulysses and Polyphemus*, after Primaticcio, 104
7. *Bookplate*, 103
8. *Judgment of Solomon*, after Rubens, 105
9. *The Visitation*, after Annibale Carracci, 106
10. *Julius Caesar*, after Titian, 107
11. *St. Rocco*, after Cherubino Alberti, 108
12. *Statuette of Neptune*, after Giovanni da Bologna, 109
13. *Descent from the Cross*, after Rembrandt, 58 (color), 112
14. *Christ and the Woman of Samaria*, 110
15. *Romulus and Remus, Wolf and Sea God*, 111
16. *The Death of St. Peter Martyr*, after Titian, 113
17. *The Presentation in the Temple (The Circumcision)*, after Veronese, 114
18. *The Massacre of the Innocents*, after Tintoretto, 115
19. *The Entombment*, after Jacopo Bassano, 118
20. *Holy Family and Four Saints*, after Veronese, 119
21. *The Mystic Marriage of St. Catherine*, after Veronese, 120
22. *The Crucifixion*, after Tintoretto, left sheet, 64 (color), 116 center sheet, 37 (proof of key block), 64 (color), 116 right sheet, 65 (color), 117
23. *Miracle of St. Mark*, after Tintoretto, left sheet, 122 right sheet, 123
24. *The Marriage at Cana*, after Veronese, left sheet, 124 right sheet, 125
25. *Presentation of the Virgin in the Temple*, after Titian, left sheet, 136 center sheet, 136 right sheet, 137
26. *The Virgin in the Clouds and Six Saints*, after Titian, 121
27. *The Descent of the Holy Spirit*, after Titian, 126
28. *The Finding of Moses*, after Veronese, 127
29. *The Raising of Lazarus*, after Leandro Bassano, 128
30. *Christ on the Mount of Olives*, after Jacopo Bassano, 38 (key block), 132
31. *Melchisedech Blessing Abraham*, after Francesco Bassano, 129

32. *Dives and Lazarus* (The Rich Man and Lazarus), after Jacopo Bassano, left sheet, 130 right sheet, 131
33. *Algernon Sidney*, after Justus Verus, 134
34. *Antique Bust of Woman*, 135
35. *Lovers* (facing right), perhaps after Piazzetta, 138
36. *Lovers* (woman full face), perhaps after Piazzetta, 139
37. *Lamentation Over the Body of Christ*, 133
38. *Heroic Landscape With Dedication and Classical Ruins*, after Marco Ricci, 140
39. *Heroic Landscape With Sheep, Statues, and Gentlemen*, after Marco Ricci, 141
40. *Heroic Landscape With Fisherman, Cows, and Horsemen*, after Marco Ricci, 40 (color), 41 (color, detail), 142
41. *Heroic Landscape with Cart and Goatherd, with S. Giorgio Maggiore in Background*, after Marco Ricci, 143
42. *Heroic Landscape with Women at Brook, Child Fishing, and Herdsmen*, after Marco Ricci, 144
43. *Heroic Landscape with Watering Place, Riders, and Obelisk*, after Marco Ricci, 59 (color), 145
44. *Battle near Parma*, after Francesco Simonini, 146, 147 (detail)
45. *Ornamental Border with Fruit, Flowers, and Purple Grapes*, 148
46. *Ornamental Border with Fruit, Flowers, and Green Grapes*, 148
47. *Ornamental Frame with Flowers and Fruit*, 149
48. *Ornamental Frame with Fruit*, 150
49. *Ornamental Frame with Flowers and Girl's Head*, 62 (color), 151
50. *Dancing Nymph with Bow and Arrows*, 152
51. *Bust of Democritus*, 153
52. *The Lion*, 154
53. *Building and Vegetable*, 63 (color), 155
54. *Statue of Apollo*, 156
55. *The Farnese Hercules*, 157
56. *Antique Bust of a Man*, 158
57. *Pheasant and Garden Urn*, 159
58. *Ruin of Garden Temple*, 160
59. *Woman Standing Holding Apron*, after S. Le Clerc, 62 (color), 151
60. *Female Statue with Fruit and Wheat*, 161
61. *Female Statue with Mask*, 161
62. *Queen with Armor and Model of Building*, 162
63. *Apollo with Lyre*, 162
64. *Woman with Shepherd's Pipe*, 163
65. *Woman with Sheet of Music and Horn*, 163
66. *Woman with Pitcher and Apron*, after S. Le Clerc, 164
67. *Old Woman Standing*, after S. Le Clerc, 164
68. *Lady with Staff*, 165
69. *Woman with Fruit and Basket*, 165
70. *Woman with Branches and Incense Burner*, 166

71. *Woman with Flowers and Vines*, 166
72. *Standing Woman, Head Turned to Right*, after Watteau, 167
73. *Lady with Fan*, after S. Le Clerc, 167
74. *Classical Female Statue*, 168
75. *Boy Looking Down*, 170
76. *Lady with a Flower*, 169

INDEX

Alberti, Cherubino, 30
Albrizzi, G. B., 26, 28, 29
Altdorfer, Albrecht, 36n
Andreani, Andrea, 10, 11, 12n, 31, 45
Annison, M., 22

Baglioni, 27, 29
Baldung, Hans, 10
Bartolozzi, Francesco, 4
Bassano, Jacopo, 32
Baxter, George, 67
Beccafumi, Domenico, 10
Berghem, Nicolaes, 45
Bewick, Thomas, 5, 9n, 16, 17, 28, 35, 49, 50
Bibbia del Nicolosi, 26
Biblia Sacra (published by Hertz), 28
Bloemart, Abraham, 22
    Cornelius, 22
    Frederick, 22
Boldrini, Niccolò, 11
Bologna, Giovanni da, 31
Book of St. Albans, 7
Brand, Thomas, 48
Bromwich, Thomas, 42
Burgkmair, Hans, 10
Businck, Ludolph, 11, 28, 45

Cabinet Crozart, 22, 23
Callot, Jacques, 4, 18, 30
Campagnola, Domenico, 44
Canaletto, 45
Carpi, Ugo da, 10, 11, 25, 26, 41, 44, 45, 51, 52
Carracci, Agostino, 32n
Caslon, William, 16

Caylus, Anne Claude Phillipe, Count de, 22, 23, 28
Chinese woodcuts, 36, 68
Coriolano, Bartolomeo, 11, 45
    Giovanni Battista, 11
Coypel, Charles, 28
Cranach, Lucas, 9
Croxall's *Aesop's Fables*, 14, 15, 31
Crozat, Pierre, 22, 23, 48

D'Arcy, Robert, 35
Darley, Matthias, 42
Dunbar, Robert, 30
    Robert, Jr., 42, 48
Dürer, Albrecht, 4, 9n, 41, 44, 52

Eaton, Edward, 49
Ecman, Edouard, 30
Edwards, George, 5n
"Ekwitz," 14
Elliot, Sir Gilbert, 50
Enquiry into the Origins of Printing in Europe (publication), 41
Essay on the Invention of Engraving and Printing in Chiaro Oscuro (publication), 43

Faldoni, Giovanni Antonio, 30
Farsetti, Filippo, 26, 27
François, J. C., 54
Frederick, Charles, 31
Fougeron, John, 49

Gauguin, Paul, 4, 54
George III, 31
Goltzius, Hendrick, 11
    Hubert, 22, 29, 45

Goya, Francesco, 4
Guardi, Francesco, 46
Gubitz, Frederich W., 67

Hogarth, William, 17
Hollis, Thomas, 48, 49

Istoria del Testamento Vecchio e Nuovo, 26

Jackson, John Baptist
    contributions to chiaroscuro and color woodcut, 5, 6, 12, 68
    critical opinions of his work, 7, 51–54
    first work in chiaroscuro, 11, 12, 23
    birth, 14
    training, 14, 15
    early work in London, 15, 17
    arrival in Paris, 17
    association with Papillon, 18–22
    association with de Caylus and Crozat, 22, 23
    Papillon's criticism of Jackson, 19, 20
    arrival in Venice, 25
    association with Zanetti, 25, 26
    first chiaroscuros in Venice, 26
    first chiaroscuro reproducing a painting, 27
    early plans for wallpaper, 30
    influence of line engraving, 29, 30
    association with Joseph Smith, 30, 31, 32
    production of the Venetian set, 31, 32, 33
    production of the Ricci set, his first prints in full color, 33, 35, 36
    use of embossing, 33, 36
    marriage, 40
    return to England, 40
    designs for calico, 40
    career as a maker of wallpaper, 40–50
    publication of *An Enquiry into the Origins of Printing in Europe*, 41
    publication of *An Essay on the Invention of Engraving and Printing in Chiaro Oscuro*, 43
    pioneer of scenic wallpaper, 46, 47
    album ascribed to him, 48
    collapse of wallpaper venture, 48, 49
    meeting with Bewick, 49, 59
    last days, 50
    Walpole's criticism, 51
Janinet, Jean François, 4
Japanese woodcuts, 4, 33n, 36
Jegher, Christoffel, 11
Jones, Inigo, 46

Kirkall, Elisha, 5, 11, 14, 15, 22, 33, 41
Knapton, George, 33

Lallemand, George, 11, 28
Lancret, Nicolas, 47
Le Blon, Jacob Christoph, 36, 39
Le Clerc, Sébastien, 18, 19, 30
Le Sueur, Nicolas, 11, 22, 23, 28, 45
    Vincent, 11, 18, 23, 45
Lethieullier, Smart, 31
Lewis, John, 23, 25
Liber selectarum cantionum, Senfel, 7n
Lorrain, Claude, 45

Mantegna, Andrea, 12n
Mariette, Pierre-Jean, 25, 26, 28
Mattaire's *Latin Classics*, 14, 31

Mellan, Claude, 30
Moreelse, Paulus, 11
Moretti, Giuseppe Maria, 25, 45
Munch, Edvard, 4, 54

Negker, Jost de, 10
Newdigate, Sir Roger, 32n

Pannini, Giovanni Paolo, 45, 46, 47
Papillon, Jean (father of J. M.), 19, 21, 22
    Jean Michel, 6, 14, 15, 18, 19, 20, 21, 22, 23, 24, 28, 35
Parmigianino, 10, 22, 26, 44
Pasquali, J. B., 32, 40
Pezzana, 27, 28, 29
Piranesi, Giovanni Battista, 46
Pond, Arthur, 33
Poussin, Nicolas, 45

Raphael, 10, 11, 22, 23, 44
Ratdolt, Erhard, 7n
Rembrandt, 4, 31, 32
Ricci, Marco, 6, 35, 36, 46, 47, 53
Robert, P. P. A., 22
Romano, Giulio, 11, 23
Rosa, Salvator, 45
Rubens, Peter Paul, 27

Sadeler, Egidius, 29
Salviati, Francesco, 44
Savage, William, 67
Simonini, Francesco (erroneously called "Simonnetta"), 42

Skippe, John, 68n
Smith, Joseph, 30, 31
Suetonius' *Lives of the Twelve Caesars*, 29, 34, 48
Swaine, J. B., 49

Tintoretto, 32
Titian, 11, 29, 32, 44
Traité historique et pratique de la gravure en bois, 6, 14, 19, 20, 21
Trento, Antonio da, 10

"Urban, Sylvanus," 41

Vallotton, Felix, 4
Velasquez, 42
Vernet, Claude Joseph, 47
Veronese, 52
Verus, Justus, 45
Vicentino, Giuseppe Niccolò, 10, 44
Villamena, Francesco, 30
Vouet, Simon, 11

Wallpaper, first use in England, 40
Walpole, Horace, 8, 31, 51
Ward, Dr. John, 49
Wechtlin, Hans, 10
Weiditz, Hans, 7n
Whistler, James M., 5n
Wouwerman, Philips, 45
Wrey, Sir Bouchier, 32n

Zanetti, Count Antonio Maria, 11, 25, 26, 45
Zuccarelli, Francesco, 46

DATE DUE